SOME THINGS THAT DON'T MAKE SENSE

A POETRY AND SHORT FICTION COMPILATION

JAMIE SANDS

CONTENTS

978-1-0670421-3-4Some Things Which Don't Make Sense (ebook)

978-1-0670421-4-1Some Things Which Don't Make Sense (paperback)

Cover design by GetCovers

Some stories previously published

SCAREKINS ARE YOUR NEW BEST FIEND!

Welcome to the Scarekins School of Cute - where everyone can be just as monstrous as they like, as long as they have friends.

Scarekins are small monsters in the form of collectable plush dolls and they're available now!

With more than 5000 Scarekins available, you're sure to find a whole new friend group that fits you perfectly. Your real-life human friends can never compare with Scarekins.

Each Scarekin is packaged individually in a glass bottle and a non-recyclable plastic bag. The plastic bag is inside a unique Scarekins branded package, so you never know who you've got until it's far too late. To remove the Scarekin from the bottle, simply speak the three magic words: BINDING - BLOODBOND - FUN!

Scarekins are so collectable, you literally can't stop at just one!

EVERYONE LOVES SCAREKINS! Did you know that Justine over the road already has a whole cemetery playset full of Scarekins who have learned to say her name? Don't you want to do better than Justine? Of course you do. Now you can. Pick up a Scarekin today! Heck, pick up a dozen!

EVERY MONTH you can choose from the *Scarekins Spooky Semester* collection. This changes month to month so be quick and grab a full set before the next semester starts.

MOTHLY

Mothly is part person and part moth, and their shiny red eyes are so bright you won't need a nightlight! Mothly can be a bit shy, but once you get to know them, they'll be a loyal fiend for life. As an added bonus, Mothy will defend you from the forces of evil.

BIRTH SIGN: Gemini

Likes: Gardening, fresh fruit, train rides and being in high places

Dislikes: Modern art, bullies, country music, long walks

HERE'S this month's limited release Scarekin buddies:

VLORD

The pint sized vampire who fits in the palm of your hand. Just be careful that he doesn't nip your fingers! Once he gets a taste for blood he's persistently pesky.

Vlord loves to stay at home during the day and go out at night, so if you're a night owl Vlord is the perfect new fiend for you.

Birth sign: Virgo

Likes: Poetry, violin music, going shopping for new clothes, boys

Dislikes: Direct sunlight, big crowds, unsolved mysteries, being alone

You can guarantee delivery of one of this month's limited release Scarekins by starting a subscription with **Scarekin Premium.** *Click below for a special deal, only available for the next hour! Remember that subscriptions last a minimum of six months - that's six guaranteed limited edition Scarekins and your chance to win the one in a million Gold Plated Scarekin.*

Tip: Scarekins are mystery bags, and we think the surprise is a big part of the fun. But what if by chance, you find yourself with the wrong Scarekin?

It can happen - open the glass bottle, bind it to yourself and then get to know it, but something's just not quite right?

Scarekins are NON REFUNDABLE.

They are also NOT RECYCLABLE

In the event that you and your Scarekin don't quite click, you have lots of options. We recommend buying more Scarekins! Scarekins are happier when they have lots of friends, and you will be too!

Limited edition monthly Scarekin:

Cindermonster

Cindermonster is the fairest of them all, a small weird thingimie who doesn't quite understand how the world works. Cindermonster needs your help to get through the day, so if you like being relied on, they might be the one for you!

. . .

BIRTH SIGN: Libra

Likes: Dancing, purple polka dots, screaming into the void, consuming insects

Dislikes: Wet socks, small dogs, loud sudden noises and chainsaws

WARNING: before opening your new Scarekin fiend, remember to remove all infants, pets and silverware from the room.

ALSO AVAILABLE CINDERMONSTER'S Dream Home playset, featuring a grooming station, sacrifice circle, bed and transforming dress.

Note: Scarekins may not come with all the accessories pictured. All playsets and changes of clothing are sold separately.

NEW RELEASE LINE of mystery bags:

ALOYSIUS

A MINIATURIZED WEREWOLF is just like a teacup poodle!

Your friends will be so jealous of how chic you and Aloysius look together on the full moon. Keep him fed with fresh wolfsbane cookies (sold separately) to keep him "healthy" throughout the lunar month. Whining is Aloysis's way of saying he loves you!

BIRTH SIGN: Taurus

Likes: Fashion, praise, gratitude lists, making art, walks under the trees

Dislikes: Coffee, spiders, blood-letting, empty notebooks, old ballpoint pens, tennis balls, gray carpet and chocolate

THERE'S nothing like a genuine Scarekin to keep your house feeling like a home, buy some today!

WHAT'S THIS? A special edition, strictly limited numbers Scarekins rare *fiend:*

[NAME REDACTED]

[name redacted] is a cheeky little beast who is very shy indeed. Once you've opened [name redacted] try your best to memorise how they look, because you might only see them very briefly from now on. [name redacted] is one of the rarest types of Scarekins!

They're a special type of [redacted] who just loves to metamorphose and listen to chill music.

BIRTH SIGN: Aquarius

Likes: Wallspace, crawlspace, dust bunnies, mouse families and playing with your hair

Dislikes: Bright sunlight, being perceived, hot coffee (ew, so bitter!)

ONCE YOU START COLLECTING Scarekins you won't be able to stop - but that's alright because why would you want to? Scarekins are the friends you never had, and they would never betray your secrets. Not to Antony even though his parents have more money than your parents. Not to

Melody, even though she has the Scarekins Nightmare Castle. No, your Scarekins will be loyal to you forever and ever.

SCAREKINS NIGHTMARE CASTLE is available now!

IT'S the perfect place for your Scarekins to dwell when you're out doing other things. Features include: Three floors of rooms for your Scarekins to play in, a working elevator, a rickety spiral staircase and a trapdoor on the ground floor leading to a spooky hidden basement. The castle comes with over one hundred random accessories! Make sure to film yourself unboxing your Scarekins Nightmare Castle so all your friends can be jealous of your haul. You could get a limited edition hat, a stretching rack, an iron maiden, one hundred Scarekins sized coathangers, or a cute new pair of boots!

Nightmare Castle is large and will fit all your Scarekins play-sets neatly inside. There's even a latch so you can close it up tight and keep your Scarekins safely contained. Before ordering, make sure you've cleared enough space in your room to house the Nightmare Castle. Some Scarekins fans recommend doing away with the boring old bookcase, or even moving your sister out into the living room so you can make the perfect space for your new Nightmare Castle. Remember, you won't need a sister once you have your Scarekins Nightmare Castle full of happy Scarekins.

BACK FOR ANOTHER ROUND?

Scarekins re-release **Freddy!** The most popular Scarekin of last season is back! You asked for it, and we listened. Grab a new Scarekins mystery box today and you might just meet Freddy.

· · ·

FREDDY THE FRESNO **Nightcrawler**

He might just look like a pair of pants with eyes but make no mistake - Freddy is a warm and friendly Scarekin who wants to get to know you better. Freddy is a great friend for people who are afraid of walking alone at night, or style-focused babes who want someone to watch Fashion Week coverage with.

BIRTH SIGN: Aquarius

Likes: Long walks in the park, thrift-shopping, unicorns, scissors, shoes, slow walks at night

Dislikes: Mud puddles, gloves, toadstools

SCAREKINS SPORTS DAY RELEASE! These Scarekins are ready to celebrate Scarekins High School Sports Day, with all the enthusiasm their little hearts can muster.

CHUCKLES

Chuckles is a recently undead pal who just wants to eat as much as they can! Make sure to keep Chuckles happy by feeding him regularly, or you might get some nibbles in the night! Chuckles is a friendly zombie, but we advise you watch your fingers!

Birth sign: Scorpio

Likes: Eating, long slow walks, the outdoors and campfires

Dislikes: Snow, sprinting races and sports days

SECURE your Secrets and your Scarekins with the awesomely spooky **Scarekins Safe**

These days a lockable diary just isn't enough. To keep your private thoughts and things secure and away from the prying eyes of parents, siblings and frenemies like Suki, make sure to get the Scarekins Safe as soon as humanly possible! The lock is triple secure with a thumbprint reader, a digital code, and a unique three word code just for you. Decorated with cute pentagrams and mystical runes. Your safe also comes with a specially selected bundle of dried herbs and candles so you can do special rituals with your Scarekin buddies.

ReveNancy

What was that sound whistling through the trees? What is that chilly feeling on your ankle? It might just be ReveNancy! ReveNancy is the most devoted fiend you'll ever meet, much more loyal and sweet than any of your so-called friends from school. You know how Cherie said that nasty stuff about you last month? ReveNancy would never do something like that to you.

Birth sign: Virgo

Likes: Long skirts and corset tops, cobwebs, dark rooms, clapping games

Dislikes: Loud noises, fish, churches, cats, dogs, small furry animals

Bernard

Bernard needs tender loving care, and daily scale polishing to stay looking his best. Your friends will be so impressed when you bring a cute little dragon to school or to a party. Bernard is very sensitive and needs to be praised frequently. Give him lots of sparkly and shiny things to hoard and he'll be contented.

Birth sign: Aries

Likes: Gold, silver, jewels, saffron, platinum, diamons barbequed meat, toasted marshmallows

Dislikes: Being alone, bare feet, vegetables

ARE YOUR SCAREKINS ACTING BORED, **sad or sluggish?**

SOMETIMES SCAREKINS NEED a bit of extra attention, or they can play a little less vigorously than usual. But don't worry! If your Scarekins friends are looking less than their best, there are simple steps you can take to get them back to one hundred per cent.

The first and easiest way is to offer your Scarekin a little blood. It can be as simple as pricking your finger, or if you're squeamish, just ask your parents or caregivers to help out with their blood. Scarekins seldom feed for longer than five minutes, and a simple boost of blood will usually perk them right back up again!

If your Scarekin doesn't bounce back after a feed of blood, you might need to download the Scarekins Grimoire and use the instructions within. A QR code to the Grimoire comes with every Scarekin purchased, and you can find it on the official website as well. Alternatively look up the official Scarekins YouTube channel for our live readings of the Grimoire, every Friday night at 7.30pm EST

REMEMBER, one Scarekin is never enough.

Scarekins aren't just for Christmas, they're for life, and they become your entire lifestyle!

YOUR NAME

Your Name is a very limited collectors edition Scarekin that you will not want to miss out on. Unlike other Scarekins, they come in a viscous FriendSac™ which must be opened in a steamy, warm room. Only you must be present on opening, as *Your Name* needs to be able to imprint on you. Created with ground breaking biological nano-technology, *Your Name* will come to life in moments.

Your Name will take on your appearance and your personality as soon as imprinting has completed. The perfect companion for the rest of your days!

FriendSac™ can be safely composted after use, or devoured for extra nutrients by you or your Scarekins

Birth sign: Whatever yours is

Likes: Everything you like

Dislikes: Everything you dislike, being left alone

2

THE QUEEN OF CUPS

The final thing was set carefully in place: a new teapot with a blue sheen, the most beautiful azure tone. The pot had a deep, powdery finish under the gloss of the glaze. She was very proud of this purchase. Especially after the last teapot had broken so dramatically.

She clasped her hands and surveyed the table set up. It was perfect, everything she wanted arranged just so; the cupcakes (rose and lemon flavours) on their pretty antique stand, the butter cookies forming a fan on their rose plate, and the cucumber sandwiches, cut in perfect triangles, waiting under a slightly damp and exceptionally clean tea towel.

All was ready.

The pulled the star-patterned cloth off the ouija board. She moved the planchette from its place beside the teapot and set it on the board, resting her fingers lightly on it, she took a deep breath. Once she was properly centred within herself, she spoke loudly to the empty room.

"Grandma, are you there? Tea is ready."

She let her breath out, and took another.

Nothing changed for a moment, but then the curtain fluttered, as if from a breeze from an open window, although the window was sheet glass and double-glazed.

THE FAINT SMELL of musk hit her nostrils and she smiled.

"This looks lovely, Marie." The warm, familiar voice crackled, staticky and slightly distance, like it was coming from a gramophone. "Thank you."

"Of course, Grandma," Marie said. "Let me pour for you."

REFLECTION

I pick up a pen, put it to paper
    Reconnect to the me of 24 years ago (and earlier)
When I thought poetry
Could change the world
When I thought poems
Would be my whole
Money-making
Career
I'd make it work

"I DIDN'T KNOW you wrote poetry"
    Well, I know enough about it

WHY NOT TAP BACK into
    That ineffable something?
    Draw from the well of ink
    And see what comes out?

FOUND POETRY FROM BOOK TITLES
IN A SECONDHAND BOOKSHOP

Wake
        Early one morning
someone else's garden
nobody but us
Tenderness
Beloved
Wild abandon
Take nothing with you
chances are
one day
secret of happiness
fire in the blood
The truth, according to us

THE FEMALE PERSUASION
Too many men
The matriach, my brilliant friend, Becky, the queen's wife, the
woman who walked into doors, the tiger's wife, the rose grower,
the girl on the train
Assembly

Big sky, Utopia Avenue
When will there be good news?
The discomfort of evening
two years, eight months and twenty-eight nights

THROUGH THE LONESOME dark
　　inland
　　the known world
　　heat and dust
　　Haven - the villa at the edge of the empire
　　Life is good
　　The girl they left behind, the way back home

THE THRILLER SECTION
　　A strangeness in my mind
　　her fearful symmetry, she's come undone
　　If nobody speaks of remarkable things
　　the dust that falls from dreams
　　Confess
　　into the blue
　　Small great things, the last wish
　　Two nights
　　the girl from Venice
　　The girl on the train
　　Colder than the grave
　　Remember me
　　Long road to mercy

SOFT BLANKET BEAR

(T*his piece is non-fiction, sorry for misleading you with the title of the book)*

MOST CHILDREN HAVE A SECURITY BLANKIE, don't they? It can be just about anything, but it becomes the thing which allows them to sleep safe at night, to feel at home, to know that things will be alright.

Mine was a woollen blanket called "Soft Blanket". I think part of me called it soft so that it would become ever so slightly less scratchy. I had it from when I was very small, I believe it was a blanket my mum put over me in my cot. Once I was walking, I would carry it around, dragging on the floor behind me and generally love it. Couldn't sleep without it.

When I was four or five years old, my mother must have got sick of watching me drag this blanket around and offered to cut it into two blankets, which I consented to - thinking it might be convenient to have one upstairs and one downstairs. But one the deed was done, I had regrets - Soft Blanket was torn asunder! (And nicely hemmed and returned to me, but that was beside the point.) I couldn't have one upstairs and one down, Soft Blanket was still one being, and I had to keep it together.

Years passed and I was still sleeping with Soft Blanket, rubbing the rough weave between my fingers, pressing my cheek against the softest bit. I was about twelve or thirteen when I began to feel entirely too grown up for Soft Blanket, I was embarrassed to still have it in bed with me, it seemed so childish, and yet I hated the thought of getting rid of it.

Around this time I also formed an obsession with teddy bears, which one might argue is still childish, but I focused my study on the history of bears, why the first one was made and sold, how they caught the imagination of children worldwide. I didn't just read about teddy bears though, I began to make them. This obsession lasted until I was almost fifteen, and somewhere in those teddy bear sewing years, I decided to convert my beloved Soft Blanket into a bear.

I was careful about it, I used a pattern that I had used before and knew worked, and I used cut up pieces of Soft Blanket as stuffing in the bears tummy, so that as much of the blanket was retained as possible. Cutting the pattern pieces out of Soft Blanket felt a little like sacrilege and a little like an echo of Mum all those years ago.

The blanket was badly worn through in places, and you can see it on the bear's chest where I sewed a heart shape to mask one of the worst places, and largely failed. The stuffing never sat right in his face and nose, but overall he's a big, huggable love of a bear, and a link to my childhood that I don't think I could ever let go of.

6

WHICH TREE

(T *hank you to Possum Creek Games for Sleepaway)*

THERE'S a tree in the woods that you shouldn't approach after dark.

If you've been up the path at the back of camp, past the ruins of the original cabin, and the ravine where the crows roost, you'll know which tree I mean.

Witch tree?

Maybe.

The tree, well, in the daytime it just feels a little colder around it; people don't tend to sit down and rest; they're more likely to move on and find another spot. But it's different at night.

Dangerous.

But I know it doesn't mean much to you if that's all I say about it. You'll just be curious and seek it out, so I'll tell you about what happened with Talia, a few summers back. If you listen nicely, afterwards I'll sing you a song.

We were playing a camp-wide game of hide and seek. A camp tradition, as you know. Only that year there were no boundaries

18

to the game, no limits to where you could or couldn't hide. So, campers were all over the place. Some hid under their cabins, some were lurking in the reeds down by the lake and some particularly brave souls were hiding behind the standing stones.

The game took hours, and it was a lot of fun. Mostly. It was getting dark as the game wound down, and most of the campers were heading to the dining hall.

I was still searching. Looking for Talia; ze was one of the last ones to be found. Ze was in my cabin and therefore my responsibility. On instinct, I took the path past where the original cabin used to stand. I found Xavin in the ravine talking to the crows, so she came with me.

I couldn't tell you what it was which drew me to the tree. Maybe my gut, but maybe another sense altogether. I didn't *want* to go there. Not after what happened with Timothy. But that was even longer ago, and another story for another night.

We saw Talia as soon as we stepped under the tree's broad canopy. Xavin pulled out a flashlight and shined it up into the tree. Talia was on a branch about twelve feet up. Zer eyes were wide but. I saw something chilling. Usually, zer eyes were mahogany brown and warm. Now they were gray. A corpse-like film over the pupil and iris. Zer face was rigid, eyes staring down at me and Xavin.

"Talia, found you!" I said, brightly as I could manage. "Come on down."

Talia's gaze pierced me, and I wanted to run. My heart thumped, rabbit instincts deep inside me telling me to get out of there. But ze was my responsibility. I had to stay.

"Come down, now."

"I don't want to jump." Talia's expression was unchanged but zer voice was desperate.

"No, don't jump, climb down."

Talia's eyes rolled to the side, towards the trunk of the tree.

There was a shadow there, something lurking. It was hard to make out anything at all, but there was definitely something.

19

"It wants me to jump." I pulled Xavin behind me and tore my eyes from the shadowed shape, focused on Talia.

"Don't listen to her. Be safe, climb on down. The way Billie taught you on the first day of camp."

Talia shook zer head. "It's in my head, Bastian! I can't — it's going to make me—"

Talia's knee twitched, then stilled. My blood froze. I spared the briefest of glances back towards the shadow. It was curled from the back of the trunk towards Talia. It could almost have been human but there were too many limbs. The head looked small, but it had a good head of Sadako-from-Ringu hair.

Talia lifted a foot, and it hovered in the air for a horrible moment before ze set it back on the branch. Ze whimpered. This kid, ze was usually fearless, bold, and outspoken. Zer whimper was heartbreaking.

I had to do something. I had to get through whatever hold the shadow had on zem. I had to keep zer talking.

"Talia. You don't have to let her do anything," I said. "Do you remember the talk we had as a cabin at the start of summer? About how only you are in charge of your body?"

There was a beat of silence. In a tiny, quavering voice, Talia replied. "Yeah?"

"No one is allowed to do anything you don't like. If they try something, what do you say?"

This was the refrain of the talk. I drilled it into them that consent was essential. They could tell people to stop. Nothing happened to their bodies that they didn't control.

"NO. STOP," Xavin said. Talia blinked.

"No, stop," Talia said, zer voice barely above a whisper.

"It's the same deal here," I said. "This thing wants to be in your head? But your head is yours. Kick it out."

"It's trying to make me jump."

"Tell it no!" I shouted. I can project my voice well, all those years of singing, and the word 'no' echoed around the branches of the tree. Whispers and hisses.

"No?" Talia's voice was too small. I swung my guitar from its customary place on my back and strummed a few notes. I had no idea what song I was about to sing, but I trusted it would come. The right song always came to me if I started to play.

THE SHADOW THING crawled off the tree's trunk and up the branch towards Talia.

"No." Talia's voice was a shade stronger. I kept my eyes on zer, heartened to see the gray film fading from zer eyes. My fingers strummed again, the first few chords from *"Fighter."* Christina Aguleira? Well, why not?

"Keep going, Talia!"

"You're not allowed in my head! I don't LIKE! IT!" Talia shouted.

The shadow thing hissed.

I started to sing, straight into the chorus, cheering Talia on.

The shadow cringed backwards, reaching out with one claw but retreating with the rest of its body.

Talia took a breath, squared zer shoulders and straightened zer spine and shouted. "Get! Out! Of my mind!"

The shadow screeched, a sound which had all the crows taking to the air, and hushed the hum of crickets entirely.

I raised my voice and sang about strength, Xavin joined in.

The shadow thing scuttled up the tree, and the rustling of leaves faded.

Talia, nimble as a monkey, swung down the branches and landed beside us, eyes clear.

I stopped playing, swung my guitar back around and crouched. "May I hug you?"

"Yeah." Ze hugged me hard, and I could feel zer body shaking. Her heart beating so hard her back vibrated from it.

We were lucky that night, we made it back to our cabin. Talia had nightmares every night for the rest of summer, maybe ze still is having them. Zer hair had turned from black to palest grey, but ze is alive, and that's what matters.

So, that's the story. I hope you all listen, and don't try your own luck when you don't need to. Now, about that song I promised to you. You all listened nicely, what would you like to hear?

7

4AM

You turn over in bed for the fortieth time
    But it's too hot that way as well
    You flip the pillow, hoping for a cool respite
    But the room itself is too warm, too close. Sultry and not in a good way
    You can feel the sweat beading between your shoulder blades and it feels inescapable
    Your blood feels sluggish and your brain feels slow
    If only you had a fan that worked, or air conditioning, but this place was cheap to rent precisely because it didn't have those things

SIGHING, you pick up your phone. The clock reads 3:58. The worst time to be sleepless
    If you don't drop off soon your mind start to spiral through memories and agonies and what ifs
    Endless replaying of cringeworthy moments
    The times you screwed up
    The people who hate you

The possibilities of what could have been if you hadn't said the wrong thing

THE HEAT IS oppressive
A glass of water might help, you think
Your mind feels unhelpful, focusing on things that wouldn't help, but water… water might help with that too

YOU ROLL OVER, sleep shirt clinging to your skin
You're half upright when you hear it
A sound you've heard dozens of times, but never at this hour
And hearing it now makes it so much more eerie
Tinkling bells of an ice cream van
Is it Greensleeves that they play?
It feels unreal
Ice cream? At this time?

BUT YOUR MOUTH is watering and you're already imagining the cool, refreshing melt of the soft serve in your parched throat
The chimes get louder
It must be right outside
So close, you could just go downstairs and have cool, delicious ice cream
Your mouth waters

YOU OPEN the curtain to look out
There, on the street below, three floors down and parked in the pool of a street light
A shiny white ice cream van
So familiar
So unexpected in the dark of night

Two people are in the street already, lining up

THAT MEANS you have time
    It wouldn't drive off while you went downstairs

YOU GRAB your wallet and keys, shove your feet into slides
    You consider pulling on a hoodie or a jacket for modesty but you can't stand the thought of another layer
    Other people can just deal with your crumpled sleep shirt and old shorts
    It's four in the morning
    They're probably dressed exactly the same as you are

THE HALLWAY LIGHTS come on automatically as you step out of your apartment
    You punch the button for the elevator and it chimes
    Impossibly loud and accusing in the sleepy building
    A thrill of embarrassment pinks your cheeks
    You're a little impressed with yourself as well
    Who are you to get ice cream from a truck on the road at four in the morning
    How adventurous it would sound when you recounted it
    How cool and devil-may-care it would make you seem

THE ELEVATOR CHIMES as it reaches the lobby and you step out, slides slapping on the marble tiles
    You have to punch the door release, it turns itself on around eight in the morning
    Hours from now
    You reach towards the button but something stops your hand, tells you to look up

The ice cream truck is over the road and although there is no traffic, it's a mere handful of steps, something in the back of your mind has issued a warning

Your blood pulses in your ears

Your body is looking for a threat

You LOOK around

There is no one but you in the lobby

There is no one on the street except for the people you saw lining up for ice cream

From this angle they are hidden by the truck itself though

The side of the truck is painted with cheery blue script that promises *cool and refreshing treats for children old and young*

There's a cartoon cone with a smiling face painted there. Eyes just a little too wide to look friendly

Your MOUTH WATERS AGAIN

Ice cream would taste so good, would be the respite from the humidity that you need so much

Cool your brain down and your body would be able to sleep

You don't need to linger after all, just buy a cone and come back inside

THE DOOR RELEASE has a satisfying give under your finger

You're impatient at your own hesitation

Try to recover the devil-may-care attitude

Ignore your pulse in your head

You walk out

You slightly regret the choice not to grab a hoodie as the fresh air is more chill and goosebumps prickle your arm

· · ·

You cross the road, clutching your wallet and look out at the printed menu of ice cream options

The person in front of you in the queue receives their cone
    Something dark red and lush looking
    A plum gelato maybe, has to be a gelato of some type
    You're surprised to see that there's no gelato on the menu when you look back at it
    All the cones pictured are vanilla soft serve

They turn towards you, cone in hand, eyes hidden behind dark glasses
    Some sort of poser
    Blonde hair long and messy
    They must have been asleep and woken up recently, or else tossing and turning the way you were
    You didn't consider the state of your hair

Your turn
    You step up to the counter of the truck and look inside
    The man in the ice cream truck frowns

"One sprinkles cone," you say. It's the first thing that comes to mind, having instantly forgotten the other options in your confusion over the gelato
    Having said it you feel suddenly infantile
    Out of your depth
    Sprinkles were a baby's choice, not a grown-ups

. . .

THE ICE CREAM man shakes his head. "The soft serve machine is ... out of order."

"But they just got a cone."

You jab your thumb over your shoulder, at the dark glasses person

"That's a special item." The ice cream man doesn't quite meet your gaze

"Okay, so can I have a special item then?"

A HAND ON YOUR SHOULDER, you startle

The grip is stronger, more of a grip than seems necessary

You turn to look into the eyes of the person who had already been served

Their dark sunglasses reflect your face back to you - you look small and distorted by the curve of the lens

"It's not for you."

THERE'S something wrong with the other person's face. Their skin is ghostly, and their lips don't seem to be able to close over their teeth

You try and pull back from their grip, to move away, but their fingers tighten and long nails dig into your shoulder

"I SHOULD -"

You were going to say 'go' but the word dies on your tongue, bloodless

The other person who had a special cone has taken off their dark glasses and you can't look away from their strange, intense eyes

One look at them and your thoughts fly from your mind, forgotten

There is nothing but the gaze, cool steel, it would relieve the heat in your veins

BOTH OF THEM have lips which are red, horribly raw like meat, maybe from eating the special item

"JUST... give me some to restock for tomorrow," the ice cream man says. "And I'll keep a look out."

The two close in on you

Fingernail-claws digging into your flesh and long fangs filling your vision

It's too warm

The hottest night of the year

But your vision goes gray as you begin finally, blessedly, to cool

8

RISE OF THE KAIJU FIGHTERS

"This way!" Piccolo led her squad up the tallest building, they moved efficiently.

"It's on our heels," Sally, the drag queen, hissed into the comms.

"Shouldn't have worn heels, then," Mushroom teased.

The team swarmed onto the rooftop and took a second to regroup.

"Don't fret." Bailey — Piccolo's trans boy crush shook his boy-band hair out of his eyes as he vaulted the safety rail. "It's a Baffer, we'll see it raise its weapon."

Piccolo refocused. "Get the tranq ready. Mushroom, did you see the weak spot?"

"Not yet, Captain." Mushroom, legal gender: *forest cryptid*, adjusted their binoculars.

"Keep us posted." Piccolo scanned the block.

The city had been cleared; the citizens now well used to the meaning of the warning sirens. Piccolo rubbed her stubble as she checked their position. Deemed it safe enough.

The Baffer, a ten-storey-high weasel-like monster with rows of teeth, hefted a gigantic mallet. It had already destroyed three city blocks downtown.

Bailey shouldered his weapon — a bazooka rigged to fire huge tranquilisers — with Sally's help. Fran, the token cis person every Kaiju Fighter squad had to include, pulled up the last of the abseiling gear.

The Baffer was getting closer.

Piccolo looked it over, catalogued what she could. Its fur was golden, ragged, and tinged with mildew — not new out of the clone factory then.

"There! Left armpit!" Mushroom cried.

"Bailey. Ready to fire?" Piccolo glanced his way.

"Ready."

The Baffer readied to attack. It grinned, a rictus, eyes narrowing like a cartoon villain. Both paws around the handle of its mallet, it raised it up.

"Firing!" Bailey called.

As always, his aim was true.

The Baffer whimpered, its mallet fell to the street, crushed several cars. The monster sagged, dropped.

"Excellent shot!"

Sally radioed in the extraction team without having to be asked.

Relieved, Piccolo saluted her squad.

Her team was first of the Kaiju Fighter squads. There were so many now, she'd lost count. But her team was still the best.

THE VAST BLUENESS

I t's a strange thing to find your house moving at over a hundred kilometers an hour.

Whipping, tearing and roaring as I cling, longing for the quietude of the days before.

MY HOME HAS ALWAYS BEEN one of the more risky types of habitat. I knew it when I moved in. The solid plastic cladding is firm and reliable, though. I'm elevated out of floods and away from dangerous things, beasts which might harm me. I enjoy the closing door. Many of my friends and siblings don't have the luxury of a door that can swing open and shut (albeit the opening doesn't open *far*). To be perfectly fair, the controls aren't mine to use, but it's of no matter, I can squeeze around the edges just fine when it's closed.

MOST OF THE time my house is dry and warm.

But sometimes it moves, goes to new places. Every so often I am overrun by a sudsy tsunami, all roading, frightening horror and the danger of being washed right out of my house and into a watery grave.

I am tough though, I endure.

Holding tight, I brace and let the water flow past.

I rebuild my webs after the destruction is over.

I AM USED to those things.

THIS WAS NEW. The high speeds. The winds whipped around my house and threatened to pull me out. It was harder to hold on. If I peeked out the crack in the door frame I could see the world whip past so fast it was nothing but a blur.

I'M MADE of stern stuff, and I braced all eight of my legs and let the shuddering shakes move through me. I had survived worse than this, although I couldn't immediately think of an incident to illustrate that notion.

A PAUSE, a slowing of movement. The roar of the engine dies out.

The loud slamming noise that indicated the giant was leaving the house's vicinity.

I SPENT SOME TIME WAITING, listening, feeling a gentle breeze that smelt new. I cautiously, slowly removed myself from my house, slipping around the door. There was nothing around. The sun shone down with warm reassurance. I climbed on top of my house and looked.

. . .

MY EYESIGHT ISN'T the best, but it's enough to know that I was somewhere I'd never been before.The house is positioned on flat hardness, and beyond that I see grass and trees in one direction. Nothing that would account to the interesting scent on the breeze. I turn slowly and see it, the cause. A vast water, repeating a soft crash and drag. Above it, birds wheel, and I keep one eye on them in case they're interested in a spider for lunch. They call out to each other in high pitched voices but do not notice me.

I INHALE. Salt, earth, something green and growing, all merge together to make this huge, moving water something unique.

I AM IN LOVE INSTANTLY.

AROUND ME A SUDDEN cloud of sandflies, silly, stupid things that I can pluck out of the air and eat my fill of. The sandflies are slow to respond, and belly full, I take in my options.

MY HOUSE IS VERY GOOD.
    But I want to stay here, and the biggest drawback now is that the house moves. I cannot control the destination, and if it were to leave this place I know I would never be the same. I must stay where this water is.

IT'S a big change for me. I've lived in this house for years, had babies there, and raised them until they could spin their own webs. It's frightening to leave a place of safety. To leave my sanctuary for the unknown, but I am too in love with the new place to let my fears overcome me. There are other cars, after all. If I decide to, I can move into another rear-vision mirror.

．．．

MIND MADE UP, I scurry down the side of the car, and over to the nearest wooden pole. There are cracks and crevices there. I choose one with a view of the vast blue water, and relax.

THE FUTURE UNFOLDS before me in the breaking of the waves and the sweet scented air. Tomorrow I will venture out, meet the locals, see what there is on offer. But for now I am more than content to view the beauty before me.

REMOTE WORKING GOTHIC

C hoi TJ signed in for another day of work in lockdown. It was tedious but it paid the bills. They loaded up the company's preferred video chat programme. The ringtone sounded. TJ was sure they'd put their laptop on silent. The call was coming from a name they didn't recognize.

Choi Phoenix.

WEIRD.

Same last name.

THEY FROWNED, checked their calendar. No meetings booked. The caller profile had no photo. TJ hesitated, then clicked on the 'accept call' button. The call quality was awful, the video blurred, pixelated, staticky.

"HELLO?" the voice sounded utterly unfamiliar.

"Hey there," TJ said. "You've got TJ."

"Thank the stars."

TJ squinted, trying to make out more than the basic details of the caller's face. Pixelated blobs of dark and less dark. "I've been trying to reach you... I-I must have got the timing wrong."

"Yeah, I just logged on."

"This is going to sound utterly unbelievable," Phoenix said. "I'm from another realm. I need to make sure you say yes."

TJ blinked. "You're right, that is not believable."

"Listen, there's a favor you have to do. You'll be asked today, or maybe tomorrow. You have to say yes."

"A favor?"

"It means you won't be in your house when the—" The call's distortion flared, feedback making TJ wince.

"When what?"

"— fair folk." The words came through clear and chilling.

"I'm hanging up."

"No, listen, I'm your wife! Husband sometimes. I need you to do this."

"Wife...what? I'm married?" TJ shook their head. This was ridiculous.

"The portal opens tonight!"

The call cut off before TJ could say another word. *Portal? Favor? Fair folk?*

LATER, TJ's neighbor texted to ask for bread and milk. They were sick, isolating.

TJ texted back 'yes' without even thinking about the call from earlier. Looking after neighbours who were sick was just the right thing to do.

THEY WERE at the supermarket when the portal opened to the Fae realm, right in the living room of their house.

UNCONSENTED ADDITIONS

Y ou're on the bus home from work, when you first notice something off.

You're standing, it's rush hour, and someone's shoulder is digging into your back every now and then. Your feet hurt.

You're not sure what it is that struck you as strange.

It wasn't a noise. You can't hear anything more than the usual *brrrr* of the motor and the *creak beep* bus noises.

There are no smells…well, there are, but you recognise them as the normal smells of a bus: unwashed people at the end of a busy day, someone's takeaway curry dinner.

You look around, trying to spot the cause of your disquiet. The people look ordinary. The usual assortment of tense-jawed office workers, students with bags under their eyes and a white-knuckled grip on their backpacks, several of them staring at one phone, retired folks with papery skin and string bags of groceries.

But there's still something tugging at you. Some soft but relentless alarm bell deep in the lizard part of your brain telling you *Watch out! Look out! Danger!*

You look out the window, and there it is. The source of the off feeling.

There never used to be a huge, rectangular, black apartment building on that hill, did there?

You try to remember, thinking back to the day before when you rode this bus route at just the same time. Or this morning, when you were sitting and going down the road in the other direction, thinking about work…

You don't recall seeing any construction in progress.

It's true that you don't exactly pay attention to every single bit of the landscape. Your attention is usually focused on your phone.

You might have missed the construction of a monolith. But if so, why did it ping at your senses just now?

You know you didn't miss any construction on that scale. There was no building there this morning.

Now there is.

It doesn't blend with the landscape at all. The depth of the black on the walls and windows seems unreal, jarring against the weatherboard houses and green trees of the suburb it's embedded itself in.

And what are those walls made of? Sort of shiny, metallic, but dull… not like any building material you've seen before, with the way the light catches and refracts it.

It's an impossible thing.

The bus turns a corner. The view of the impossible building is gone. Hidden by the new direction of the bus, the yellowing foliage of the trees lining the street.

Your stomach is a knot of tension. You look around the other passengers, but nobody seems to have noticed, or if they have, they're not concerned.

Is it something only you can see?

Your stomach knots tighter and you feel your breath coming quicker.

The bus pulls into a stop and you get off. Trying not to stumble over your own feet, you make your way home. Your house is cold and dark, none of the flatmates are home. Which is weird but not entirely unheard of.

The house is over a hundred years old, drafty. You move around the common areas putting on lights even though the sun hasn't completely set. It makes the house feel warmer.

You're sitting down to watch the next show on your streaming playlist when you hear it.

Russika russika russika

Movement in the kitchen.

You turn your head to look but nothing seems out of the ordinary. Heart speeding up, you stand again, walk into the kitchen, switching the light on. The rustling stops.

A mouse?

You open the pantry door. Nothing there but food.

You look in the adjoining dining room and it happens again

Russika russika

Definitely behind you. You whirl around and see a skittering shape, a small pink thing.

Pink? Mice aren't pink. Not when they're full grown... and didn't it look larger than a mouse? More like a pink rat? But there wasn't a tail.

It hurried along the skirting board and vanished below a drawer. Your hands shake as you pull the drawer out entirely and set it on the floor. Whatever it was should be in the space left underneath. There's nothing there.

Letting out a heavy breath you pull out your phone and send a voice message to your flatmates. "Hey, where is everyone? I think we have a mouse situation."

It's a busy thread, someone usually responds instantly, but tonight there's nothing. Not even a 'read' notification.

It's probably nothing.

They're probably just busy. You decide to try and forget about the rustling pink rat, put the drawer back and make yourself dinner. The rice cooker lives on a shelf above the kitchen counter. You reach up to take it down and there's a *whoosh*. A thousand tiny green insects scatter.

Skitter screet skitter skiss

"What the..."

Your house gets the odd cockroach or spider now and then, but this is the first time you've seen anything like this many bugs inside. It startles you, and you drop the rice cooker. The *clang* echoes through the house.

The bugs scale the walls, hiding in the cracks in the painted plaster. You take a breath, try and get a good look at one of them. It doesn't look like any bug you've ever seen. Aren't insects supposed to have six legs? These all have four. They have large purple eyes and a sort of crest running down their back. Each of them is about the size of your thumbnail. They all vanish after ten seconds, and you're left bewildered. Did you really only count four legs?

You think you did.

What can it mean?

Dinner forgotten, you go into the lounge and switch on the TV and the news is playing. Buildings, just like the one you saw on the bus home, appear in footage from all over the country. One appears on the hill over the capital city, looming, watching. One in the countryside, odd and solid in the middle of a dried out field of wheat. One next to a new housing development just out of your town.

The news anchors are saying no one knows where they came from, that they appeared suddenly, in the middle of the day.

The footage stops and you're back watching the news anchor. You watch as they try and maintain a calm demeanor but the very fact you know that's what they're trying to do means they're failing.

"We have also had reports of strange animal sightings," the news anchor says. "Odd coloured insects and small vermin. These reports seem to have begun at the same time as the mysterious buildings' appearance, but we're unable to confirm if this is simply—"

The news anchor who wasn't talking falls out of shot. You catch a glimpse of a pale aqua form, the size of a ferret and with the same long body shape, crawling up his neck. The news feed cuts off, replaced by a network disruption notice.

Russsika russika russika

The rustling is coming from the couch beside you.

You stand up quickly.

Eyes still on the TV, you switch channels and find a live feed from a street in your city. The reporter seems distracted.

"Some say the buildings descended slowly from the sky," she glances around. You can see the dark form of a human body behind her. "Some are saying it's simply a mass hallucination, perhaps caused by the Covid-19 vaccines, but that's what people are always blaming things on now. There's no evidence. What we know is…"

She swallows and looks back at the camera, her expression stony. "It's not safe out on the streets tonight. Please, stay home, and make sure your doors and windows are sealed. Once they get inside, it doesn't seem like-"

Skitter screet skisssss

The green things have followed you. They're making a double line, curving around the doorframe and marching towards you halfway up the wall. At head height. There are so many of them.

You run to the bathroom, slamming the door behind you. You have your phone clutched in one hand and the TV remote in the other. Your knuckles are white.

What do you do next? The bathroom light shows no obvious intruders. There's a small gap below the door, you shove your flatmate's towel against it, wedging it shut, sealing the room. The window is closed. Your stomach clenches as you scan the room again. The ventilation fan. Could they get in through there?

You fire off messages to your friends, asking for help. You message your closest family, tell them you love them.

Maybe this is all a hallucination, but you feel the first touch of the green bugs on your elbow as real as anything. Aliens, somehow, seem like a more plausible explanation than hallucination.

You get no responses to any of your messages.

A lilac purple, furred beast, about a foot tall, with a long nose and tiny hands removes the fan cover from inside the vents and swings down, agile as a monkey. Another appears at the window.

Cornered.

Weaponless.

It's up to you if you scream or not.

12

END OF THE RAINBOW

Jonny's feet hurt. His sandal straps were cutting in and the soles were hard on the undersides of his feet. It was much colder than when he'd set out from the back garden. He stopped and looked back. There was nothing behind him but rocky grey path. He had long ago lost sight of his house. Jonny sighed; there was nothing for it but to keep walking.

He hoped he'd reach the end of the rainbow soon ad the leprechaun, or unicorn, or whatever was supposed to be waiting there would zoom him home. The mystery of what exactly he would fine at the end of the rainbow had got him this far; it could get him further. It could get him right to the end.

When Jonny had told his father where he was going, he'd laughed at him, and said something like 'philosophy killed the cat', but Jonny didn't believe that. A car had killed the cat. Jonny had found the body in the gutter the other morning, cold and still and stiff.

Mum had put it in a shoebox and buried it in the back garden. Besides, with all the conviction his seven years on earth could muster, he knew there were real magical creatures out there. There was *actual magic* that you couldn't explain with wires and mirrors like stuff on TV, or clever editing like the videos on Mum's phone. The real trick was you had to be in the right place when the magic happened.

The trees bordering the path were getting taller as he walked on. They loomed over him, blocking out the late afternoon sunshine and making the air even colder. He stuck his hands in his pockets to let the trees know he didn't care what they did.

Jonny heard a noise. He whistled to show the noise just how very much it didn't bother him, but he hadn't quite got the hang of whistling yet, so he just made a little half 'whoo' sound. Then he thought perhaps whistling would draw attention to him, attention he didn't want.

The noise continued, a rustling from the trees, following behind him on the left-hand side. He looked over his shoulder but he couldn't see anything but path. The noise was now definitely keeping pace with his steps. He shouldn't have whistled, but he had, and now he had to deal with it.

"I don't know who you are, and I don't care! Don't follow me!"

The rustling stopped. There was a sound like a twig breaking. The silence felt slightly offended.

"I mean it," Jonny said. "I'm cold and tired and I'm in no mood to be followed. If you keep following me where I can't see you, I'll hit you." The threat was scary to say. He knew hitting was something you mustn't do. Jonny swallowed, hoping he didn't really have to hit anyone.

Something moved in the corner of Jonny's vision, and then there was a dog-thing on the path, looking at him with huge, wild eyes.

Jonny backed away. In his hurry his sandal caught on a rock, and he fell hard, right on his bottom.

The dog-like thing came closer.

"Go home!" Jonny shouted as loud as he could. His voice wavered, but he knew that was the thing Mum said to dogs out wandering on their own.

The dog-like thing cocked its head to the side.

Jonny's fear faltered, slightly. "I don't want to hit you," he said. "Please just go home."

"I don't want you to hit me," it said.

"I don't want you to bite me," said Jonny.

"Biting people is scary. It's all hard and painful, and then they hit you. I don't bite people anymore."

"All right then." Jonny picked himself up and dusted off his shorts. "Why were you following me?" He took a closer look and saw the thing wasn't a dog at all, It was taller than Jonny and its fur had a feathery quality to it. Its eyes were large and green as the new spring leaves on the tree outside Jonny's bedroom window. Its feet were huge too, round like dinner plates.

"I HAVEN'T SEEN anyone like you on this path for a long time," it said.

Jonny nodded. He'd never been down the path from his back garden this far and he was sure his parents hadn't either. He rubbed his arms; it was really cold now. He longer for his sweat-shirt, or better, a hot chocolate in front of the heater, his mother bundling a blanket around his shoulders. "I'm going to the end of the rainbow," he said. But it was very dark now, and as he looked up he realised there was no rainbow left in the sky. His stomach turned over uneasily, but he still had the path, and he had a friend now. He looked back at the dog-thing. "I'm Jonny, what's your name?"

The thing made a woofing noise, which to Jonny sounded a bit like "Ruff", so he made that its name and together Jonny and Ruff walked the path for what felt like hours.

Ruff stayed close to Jonny's side, and he wasn't so cold anymore, and when twig goblins jumped out and tried to scratch him, he would have fallen over again and maybe even cried, except that Ruff backed and growled impressively, seeming to double in size, and showing huge glistening fangs. The twig goblins ran away.

Jonny was so tired he was having trouble keeping his eyes on. He was half-leaning on Ruff now, his shoulder pressed into the soft, feathery fur. His feet were the sorest they'd ever been in his whole life, and his legs were the coldest in the whole world because he couldn't press them into Ruff's fur and keep walking.

He was wishing very hard for his bed, and a cuddle from Mum. He'd just meant this to be a quick adventure, but now it felt like he was running away, and it was too hard and too awful. He stumbled on a rock and fell, skinning his knee, and the tears flowed down his face. It was hopeless. He couldn't even turn back now, it was so far to go.

"We're almost there," Ruff said, leaning against Jonny to share some body heat. Jonny nodded and pulled himself up again, one hand in Ruff's strange hair, as they walked. It was as comforting as his teddy bear, back home.

The trees slowly began to thin, become less scary, less dark-and-twisty and more green-leafy-friendly. Jonny's tears gradually dried up. A spring came back to his step.

The path brightened as a glowing light grew, as if the trees that lined the path were full of glow worms or fireflies. Jonny could hear soft singing.

A door opened in the path in front of him, and the light from it was as comforting as the nightlight he was too big to use anymore, although Dad still left it on if there was a thunderstorm. Together, he and Ruff went through the door. Surely, now, they were at the end of the rainbow.

There was a bed for him, certainly, and a beautiful lady wrapped him in the softest blanket he'd ever felt, and he warmed up again very fast. Ruff curled in a circle at the foot of the bed, tame as a lapdog. Strange and beautiful creatures with wings and haunted eyes gathered to tell Jonny how brave and strong he had been.

"You can rest now," their voices said, rasping and quiet. "You're safe, you'll have whatever you desire."

"Is there gold?" Jonny asked, his voice a mumble, mostly asleep.

"All the gold you need," the voices said.

Jonny caught one last glimpse of the world his parents inhabited before the door to the path closed forever, and he fell asleep.

13

HAPPY CHRISTMAS MORNING

Carrie's eyes flew open, her heart was pounding.

It was Christmas morning. It had to be, because yesterday was Christmas Eve and now it was a whole new day.

It was still very early. Carrie knew it was early because it was still dark, she couldn't see much of her room.

There was a bit of light coming from under her curtain, but Carrie thought it was probably the ambient night light.

Carrie lay in bed, paralysed with excitement. It was Christmas at last, after all the waiting and the wishing and the agony. Carrie had spent all of December preparing for Christmas. So many hours making gingerbread with her mother, decorating the Christmas tree, drawing cards and writing Merry Christmas inside them and putting them into envelopes for her friends at school.

Last night had been the hardest.

Carrie and her parents had sung Christmas carols, although her father didn't know some of the words, and they had watched *A Christmas Carol* on the vidscreen, which was wonderful, even if the setting was strange and old.

Carrie hadn't been a little bit sleepy even when it was an hour after her bedtime.

But that was over now, it was Christmas morning. Carrie pulled the curtain back, slid her feet out of bed, moving as quietly as she could manage. She slipped her feet into her bunny slippers, pulled on her dressing gown and slowly, ever so slowly, crossed the room to her bedroom door.

She'd long ago mastered the art of opening her door silently.

First, she picked up Mr Squiggleberry, her teddy bear, and smushed him over the speaker box. That way the beeping that her door did to let people know it had worked would be smothered. Second, she put her towel along the floor so that the door wouldn't make a banging noise when it slid open.

The doors weren't supposed to bang like that, but their section of the station wasn't as new as it had been. Her mother sometimes said it was falling apart, but Carrie's father said she was overreacting, and it wasn't that bad.

The door opened and thumped gently against the bunched-up towel end. Carrie snuck out into the shared habitation area.

The Christmas tree was still lit up, the fairy lights glowing red, purple, blue and yellow. Under the tree sat the presents Carrie already knew about, the small green plastic wrapped packages that her parents had put under there a week ago and which she had spent a long time carefully feeling. She had guessed what each one of those was.

Carrie looked over by the wall, where she had hung her stocking. The stocking was one of her old microfiber boot liners that she'd grown out of. The terrain outside the station was still not completely terraformed, so she had to have extra layers. Mum said they were "required". The stocking was bright green and Carrie had painstakingly sewed on it a yellow star cut out from one of her mother's old shirts.

The stocking was bulging and there was something sticking tantalisingly out of the top. Carrie stood and stared, overwhelmed with anticipation. She hoped it was the stuffed pony she'd asked for. Carrie was bursting with a need to look in the stocking, but her parents had forbidden her to touch it until they were awake.

There was only one thing to do.

Carrie ran to her parents' bedroom door, scanned her thumbprint, and burst into the room.

"It's Christmas! It's Christmas!'

They didn't move immediately so she jumped up onto the bed and onto her father's shoulder. "Wake up, wake up, Santa came!"

Carrie's mother moaned and rolled over to blink at her. "What time is it?"

"It's Christmas time!" Carrie said.

Her father rolled under the blanket and she slipped down between the two of them.

"S'not even oh six hundred," her father sounded groggy.

"Santa came! Can I open my stocking now?" Carrie nudged her mother's arm. "Can I?"

'Okay sweetie, go back to the lounge, we'll be up in a moment. Just look at the tree for a bit 'til we get there."

Carrie slid back off the bed and ran back into the shared habitation area.

She knew her mother called it a lounge because of that's one of the words they used back on Earth, but to her it would always be the SHA. Carrie sat on the cushioned seating units and bounced up and down, she looked back at her parent's room every couple of seconds. She could see them get out of bed, pulling on their dressing gowns and talking. She couldn't hear what they were saying.

Finally, they came into the SHA.

"Can I have it now?" Carrie asked.

"I need coffee," Carrie's mother said. "Wait until I have my coffee."

"Awww," Carrie couldn't help but pout.

Her father sat down next to her. He stretched one tentacle out, reached across the room and wrapped the tip gently around her stocking. He unhooked it and drew it back over to the seat without even standing up.

"You can hold it," he said, "but you can't take anything out til Mummy gets back, all right?"

"Thanks Dad." Carrie cuddled into her father's side, balancing the stocking on her lap. He laid one tentacle across her shoulders, hugging her close.

Carrie listened as the kettle boiled and her mother manipulated the mysterious machine that produced coffee. She came back in, holding two steaming mugs. She gave one to Carrie's father and sat down on the other side of Carrie.

"Go on then, let's see what Santa brought you."

Later, when Carrie had torn the paper off all her presents and given the gifts she'd made to her parents, and they'd had breakfast and Carrie was dressed they had a moment of quiet.

"This is nice," Carrie's father said.

"My advent calendar!" Carrie shouted, ruining the tranquillity. "I haven't opened today's window!" She leapt up from the seating unit, ran across to the communicator and picked up the battered cardboard. It had a big picture on the front, of an apartment building in one of the old Earth cities. There were people on the street outside it, walking with plastic bags full of presents. There was a Santa in one corner, ringing a bell. Her mother had called the picture 'quaint' but Carrie thought it was beautiful, she loved to look at all the things in the windows, like the old fashioned televisions and the optometrist shop that sold glasses.

She ran her fingers over the picture, looking for the one unopened window. There, with the number '25' on it, she pulled it open and looked at the tiny drawing underneath. "It's some people looking at a baby," Carrie said.

"It's the birth of Jesus," Carrie's mother said.

"Not this again," Carrie's father said. Carrie looked up, he had sounded annoyed. His skin was turning a darker shade of purple, which meant angry.

"Don't be like that, darling," Carrie's mother said. "It is the reason why we have Christmas. I mean, his name is right there in the title."

"It's archaic and strange, putting weird ideas in her head," Carrie's father said. He got up to look out the window at the endlessness of space.

Carrie tried not to cry, she hated it when her parents fought and this was Christmas day, they should all be happy.

Carrie's mother could see Carrie's chin wobbling and held out her arms to her.

"Well, that's how it started out," Carrie's mother said. "But it's not really why we do all this."

Carrie climbed up onto her mother's lap, clutching the advent calendar. She wished she'd never opened the stupid last window.

"Why do we do Christmas then?" Carrie asked.

Her father turned to look at them, clearly wondering the same thing.

"Because it's good to let people know how much you love them," Carrie's mother said. "Christmas is a time to do that."

"But surely we should do that every day," Carrie's father said. "Why would you restrict that to one day in 365? Why not just treat each other nicely?"

"Humans aren't very good at that, I'm afraid," Carrie's mother said. Carrie leaned back into her arms, listening hard. "We forget, we get grumpy and we treat each other badly. We have wars and take each other for granted. We have Christmas to remind ourselves that we can love each other as well."

"Hmph," Carrie's father said.

"And of course, it's nice to have a reason to get dressed up and eat a lot of delicious food," she tickled Carrie, making her laugh. Carrie had been asking about the Christmas feast all month.

"Well, I can't disagree with you there, the feast part of it is pretty amazing," Carrie's father said. He looked at his wife and child and smiled at them. "Of all the human traditions you brought with you this is the strangest, but I guess I can get into it."

Carrie leaned over and gave her father a kiss on his long rubbery face. "Merry Christmas daddy," she said.

"Merry Christmas kidlet," he said. "Come on, time for the rest of the presents."

Carrie jumped down from the seating unit and sped over to the Christmas tree to sort out which presents were for her.

"You think this is strange? I must've never explained about Easter to you," Carrie's mother said.

"Hmmm?" Carrie's father tilted his head to one side.

"A giant rabbit brings chocolate eggs."

Carrie's father just looked at his wife uncomprehendingly and then he smiled. "You're joking."

14

WAIHEKE CHRISTMAS

"I don't understand, why don't you visit your folks more often? They're so close!" Sebastian shouldered a pink and blue striped backpack full of clothes, and then picked up his leather satchel of camera gear in the other hand and carried them out the door.

"Oh, I mean, getting into town takes a while, and then the ferry is an hour or so. It's always such a hassle. I can't just visit for a couple of hours, I have to spend the night, and then I've always forgotten something or..."

He trailed off as he stepped out on the front stoop. Sebastian was looking at him with wide, adoring eyes, the expression that that Basil had come to recognise. His aura had gone all amused and affectionate too.

He's about to say I'm adorable for something ridiculous I've said or done.

"You're adorable," he said. "You can say you don't like visiting them, it's okay. I'd be avoiding my parents if they were in the country."

"I'm not avoiding them, as such," Basil said. He checked the wards on the front door and found them intact. "I like to stick around my home." In a soft voice, he whispered an additional

55

charm into the door. "Goodbye house, don't let anyone else in until we come back."

He turned to look at Sebastian who was balancing a number of bags and trying not to drop anything as he slid his sunglasses on.

"The bus to the ferry terminal must be almost due," Basil said. He took a bag off him and shouldered it. "Let's hurry."

$\sim$

THE FERRY over to Waiheke took a little over an hour, and Sebastian loved every second of it. He kept dragging Basil to different parts of the boat to take selfies.

It had been almost two months since they'd officially started dating and Basil was only just beginning to understand what he was supposed to do in a selfie.

The weather was absolutely stunning, and from the deck of the ferry the sky arced over them, a glorious clear azure, a tiny fluffy white cloud here and there. It was windy on deck though, the ferry moved quickly enough that it could get quite cold even in the balmy weather.

Basil felt the wind blow away his cobwebs and felt a surge of excitement. He used to take this trip several times a week, to university and back... staying at friend's place overnight and coming back in the morning.

Until he'd found a nice flat going cheap and moved out.

It felt like coming home still, even though he didn't visit often. The sea spray, the sunshine and Sebastian by his side bolstered him up.

$\sim$

THEY DISEMBARKED from the ferry with Basil tugging the suitcase full of gifts and Sebastian with the bags on his shoulders.

"You sure we shouldn't have booked a car?" Sebastian said, looking over at the rental place wistfully. Basil shook his head.

"No, I told Mum which sailing we are on they'll be-" A shrill voice cut through the noise of the crowd. And Basil turned to see a woman he knew in her seventies approaching with a wide lipsticky smile. His "aunt" Majorie.

"Basil! Darling, there you are, oh it's good to see you." Marjorie enveloped Basil in a hug which smelt like vanilla and patchouli. Most of Waiheke probably smelled like patchouli.

"Yes, hello," he said, hugging her back. "Good to see you, too."

"Oh you have to take a look at my herb garden, the lemon balm, you're absolutely going to lose your head." She released him and he smiled and nodded. He was about to introduce Sebastian but he was already talking.

"It's so good to meet you," Sebastian said. He'd dropped the bags on the cracked asphalt and wrapped his arms around Marjorie. "Basil's told me so much about you!"

"I have?" Basil asked.

Marjorie hugged him back warmly. "You must be Basil's boyfriend."

"Yes. Sebastian. You really raised him well," Sebastian said.

"Oh, this isn't my mother," Basil said. Marjorie laughed and let go of Sebastian. "This is aunt Marjorie, only she's not a blood relative or anything, she's an old family friend."

"Not that old!" Marjorie laughed, picked up one of the bags and smiled at them both. "Come on, car's this way, and then you can meet Basil's actual parents."

Sebastian appeared to be blushing under his sunglasses so Basil kissed his cheek before they got into the car.

"I feel a little silly," he said.

"It's fine," Basil said, squeezing his hand. "I'm sorry I wasn't quick enough to introduce you. No harm done."

Sebastian's smile was on the tight side, but once they were in the car, Marjorie launched into a long diatribe about all the local gossip for Basil's benefit. He tried to make the appropriate noises at the right time, but it was a struggle to keep up when he was still worrying about how Sebastian and his parents were getting on.

"And my daughter, Sue, you remember she moved back here from Hamilton?" Basil wasn't sure he did remember that.

"Mmhm," he said, gamely.

"Well, she's got involved in this yarn bombing circle, and the things they do are just divine, you won't believe it. Look, you can see it on the fence over there!" Marjorie pointed out the window as they drove past a house with a tall chicken wire fence, keeping in a handful of chickens. The fence had been decorated with wool, threaded through the wire to make a series of cross stitch roses in red and pink. The effect was rather charming.

"Very pretty," he said, meaning it.

In the back of the car, Sebastian was holding up his phone to the window trying to get a photo.

"We can come back and look at it again," Basil said. "You'd get a better photo from the side of the road than a moving car."

Sebastian lowered his phone and gave Basil one of his brightest smiles. "I want to record everything from Basil and my first Christmas together."

Marjorie chuckled.

"Here we are, Surfdale." Marjorie's phone beeped and she looked at the incoming message and frowned. "Hm, it's from Sue, I'd better go see her."

"I hope nothing's gone wrong?" Basil said.

"Just yarn bombing drama. I won't come in now, but I'll be by your parents' Christmas Eve get together of course," Marjorie said. She leaned over and kissed Basil on the cheek.

"Thank you so much for driving us," Basil replied. "Very much appreciated."

"Of course, now get in there, they'll be dying to meet this

one." She shook his thanks off with a shoulder twitch and pointedly revved the car engine.

Basil and Sebastian piled out, got their bags out of the rear of the car and waved as Marjorie drove off. Then Basil turned to look at the path leading up to his parent's place. The section had been subdivided in the 1920s and the path to their house wound around the front section. He shouldered a bag, gave Sebastian a tight smile and led the way.

"It's up here."

The path was, as ever, in disrepair. His parents cared very well for their house and the garden, but the path never seemed to matter quite as much. The white wooden fence jutted over the bank at an odd angle, and the concrete paving had cracked, forming an uneven slope up the hill. The lemonwood trees dotted here and there on the right and the tree ferns which grew lower to the ground on the left were overgrown, making the path even narrower. Basil made a mental note to do something about it later on.

Sebastian followed gamely, yanking the rolling suitcase over the cracks and bumps. "They must have a great view," he said.

"Oh, it's quite nice," Basil said. "But there's plenty of houses with nicer ones, especially further round the island. There's a vineyard on top of a cliff which looks right across the harbour to Auckland, it's absolutely beautiful."

"I'll have to take you to dinner there," Sebastian said. A little of Basil's nervousness was lost in the wash of pleasure that sentence brought him.

"That would be lovely." They turned the last corner of the path and Basil caught sight of the modest weatherboard house and felt more relaxed from the sight of the white walls and sea green roof. He might be embarrassed by his parents, but at least he loved them and he knew that they loved him. The feeling was short lived.

"Basil!" His father emerged from the overgrown rosemary

bush, startling Sebastian, he had leaves caught in his hair and his eyes shone behind plastic safety goggles. "You're home!"

"Hi Dad," Basil lowered his bag to the ground and went to give his father a hug. He smelled of Rosemary of course, but also fresh mint. He broke the hug to gesture Sebastian forward. Sebastian was already beaming, his eyes shiny behind his sunglasses. He was a tall man, with a receding hairline and smile lines around his eyes.

"Dad, meet Sebastian, my boyfriend. Sebastian, this is my dad Russ."

Russ opened his arms and Sebastian enthusiastically hugged him. "Good to meet you, lad," Russ said.

"You've done such a great job raising Basil," Sebastian said as they stepped away from each other again.

Russ's mouth quirked up and he chuckled. "If you like the basil you should see what I can do with parsley!"

Sebastian laughed and Basil didn't know if he was doing it to be polite. Basil himself groaned. "Dad, no dad jokes, please."

"No promises. It's Christmas, at the very least there will be the jokes in the Christmas crackers."

"I'm so happy you were okay with him bringing me for the holidays."

"Of course, make yourself at home. I believe your mother's making pizzas for dinner, go on in, I'll finish up in here and be right after you." Russ disappeared back into the rosemary bush.

Well, that could have gone worse, I suppose.

"Thanks Dad," Basil picked up the bags and led the way up and through the front door. The house didn't look like much from the front, another old New Zealand house, like all the others in the area. "Hello!" he called out as he stepped into the house.

"Hello!" his mother replied from the kitchen. "I'm in here!"

"The bags and things can go in my room," Basil opened the door to the spare room which he always used and they stashed the bags.

Sebastian had pushed his glasses up onto the top of his head and neatly stacked the bags against the wall, his eyes roaming all over the room, taking it all in. The room had good afternoon light, and the bed was covered with an old patchwork quilt, faded but still pretty. One wall was entirely bookshelves, installed at his insistence when he'd become a teenager. Most of the shelves were empty of the books he'd stored there, since he'd moved out with them, but there were still a few second hand paperbacks of science fiction and fantasy, and his mother had filled at least two shelves with mystery novels.

The rest of the shelves were given over to shallow trays of seedlings in various stages of sprouting.

Sebastian had fixated on a poster on the wall over the bed though, and Basil felt his cheeks warm. "Oh god, I meant to take that down like, ten years ago and I just never got around to it," he said. The poster showed Legolas from the Lord of the Rings movie, bow in hand, eyes fixed on the camera, smouldering.

Sebastian grinned at him, showing all his teeth. "You had a crush on Orlando Bloom?"

"I was gay, and I like neatness, what do you expect?" Basil huffed, but he wasn't really angry.

"Maybe I should learn archery?" Sebastian teased, nudging him in the ribs with his elbow. Basil imagined Sebastian pulling back an arrow - the way it'd make his arms flex, and hummed happily.

"Maybe you should."

"I was more an Aragorn fan, myself," Sebastian said. He slipped his arm around Basil and kissed his cheek. "All that scruff."

"I'm not scruffy at all..." Basil said, suddenly concerned.

"You're also not an eighty-year-old king who commands ghosts," Sebastian said. "Well, I suppose you did quite well with that one ghost."

"Come on, we'd better go say hello to my mother before she comes looking for us," Basil said, quickly, before he had to do something like push Sebastian onto the bed and kiss him until he couldn't catch a breath.

They made their way to the kitchen, recently renovated after his father nearly set fire to the house with their old oven. Basil's mother, Dawn, had made an utter mess of it. She turned as they walked in, her grey hair in disarray, mostly pulled back in a messy bun, her eyes bright and her cheek smudged with flour.

"Basil, darling!" she made for him and then caught sight of Sebastian a half step behind and changed trajectory. "Oh you must be Sebastian, my, aren't you a handsome one, good work son!"

She wrapped her arms around Sebastian who laughed and returned it. "That's very kind of you, I think Basil's better looking though."

Basil blushed and dithered, and when his boyfriend and mother were done hugging and sizing each other up, he took Sebastian's hand and gave it a squeeze.

"I'm sorry I didn't catch your name," Sebastian said.

"Just call me Dawn," she said, waving her hand dismissively. "And you're welcome to anything you like in this kitchen. It's usually Russ's domain but I wanted to make pizzas to welcome you. I'm rolling out the dough and then you can pick what you want on it, and we'll head outside to have drinks while they cook. Sound good?"

"It sounds amazing, Dawn, can we do anything to help?"

"No, you go unpack, get your presents under the tree so Russ can snoop around them, I'll call when it's time."

They left the kitchen and Dawn followed them, still talking. "How was the ferry ride over?"

"It was really smooth," Basil said.

"I got some great photos, I can show you if you like?" Sebastian said, pulling out his phone.

Russ came in the front door and all four of them stopped in front of Basil's room. Dawn looked over his shoulder and saw their suitcases.

"Honestly, Basil, if you'd kept up with your craft more, you could've saved the ferry fair and come over by some other means," his mother shook her head and Basil swallowed, feeling guilty.

"Yes, uh, you're right I'm sure."

Sebastian looked as if Basil had kicked his puppy. "I gave up bubble tea for a whole month to save up for this trip…"

"Well, I mean, the ferry tickets aren't that much…"

Dawn tsked her tongue against her teeth and shook her head at Basil. Russ patted Basil's shoulder. "With all the luggage these two brought? I don't think even all three of us could realistically have made that trip with our powers combined."

It was meant to make Basil feel better, he thought, but it didn't. He bit his lower lip and swallowed.

"Right, well, I'll uh, yeah, we'll get out the presents, and…"

Dawn gave Basil a peck on the cheek. "We worry about you, is all, sweetheart."

"I've been better with practicing since Halloween," Basil said, half heartedly. "The library ghost."

"Come on, leave them to it," Russ said, taking Dawn's elbow and turning her back to the kitchen. "Is the woodfire going already?"

"Yes, of course it is," she said, and they left Basil and Sebastian alone. Basil bit his lip and turned to Sebastian.

"Sorry about your bubble tea."

Sebastian shook his head, and his slightly overgrown curls bounced into his forehead in a particularly adorable way. "That's okay. It's just drinks." His attention caught by something over Basil's shoulder. "No way, is that a photo of teenage Basil?"

"Oh Goddess, I hope not," Basil said, turning to look. Sebastian pushed past him and picked up the framed picture of Basil, aged seventeen, down by the ocean. His hair down to his shoulders as he explored his hippie roots, his feet dug into the sand, grounding. He wore a particularly terrible pair of tie dyed shorts.

"This is adorable!"

"It's..." Basil sighed. "Well, I'm glad you think so."

"There must be so many treasures like this in the house..."

"Let's just... unpack, before you go hunting for my naked baby pictures," Basil said. He slipped his hand around Sebastian's waist and tugged, hoping to distract him.

Sebastian turned and smiled wide, pressing his chest to Basil's and kissing him enthusiastically.

Basil put his other arm around him and kissed him back, some part of him wishing they could spend the Christmas break kissing instead of all of the rest of it. Sebastian's lips were warm and soft, and he was clean shaven, his skin smooth and smelling faintly of mint. And even though they had probably kissed a thousand times by this point, it still filled Basil's heart with warmth and made his fingers tingle with excitement. He could never be bored of kissing Sebastian.

Finally, Sebastian broke away and rubbed his nose softly against Basil's. "Come on, I want to see what a witch's Christmas tree looks like."

~

THE CHRISTMAS TREE didn't disappoint, so far as Basil could tell from Sebastian's reaction.

It was plastic, since Russ hated to cut down actual trees if it could be avoided. Some of the branches had lost a fair bit of their fluffy plastic needles, but Russ and Dawn had made up for it with bundles of dried herbs tied onto the boughs with coloured twine.

It was decorated with the same ornaments Basil had seen every Christmas his entire life. He looked for his favourite - a green and pink felt Christmas stocking with an orange bird tucked inside. Dawn had sewn it for him when he was seven, and convinced he would learn how to shape shift into a bird. He found the ornament hanging towards the back of the tree, removed it and moved it to the front.

"Is this like, a charm against evil? Does it protect the tree? I'm guessing the herbs are all chosen for the same reason..." Sebastian said. He'd been crouching on the ground, carefully arranging their gifts for each other and Basil's parents at the foot of the tree. Basil looked down to see him pointing at a haphazard stick and wool thing Basil had made in his first year of school.

"No, that's a school project." Basil shrugged. "As for the herbs," he paused to look over the various bundles. "Well, some of them have protective properties but I expect my parents mostly chose them because they look and smell nice inside. We don't usually charm the tree."

"Oh," Sebastian said, sounding disappointed.

"I mean, not *everything* in the house is magical..." Basil said. "But some of it is." He felt bad for disappointing Sebastian, so he took his hand and led him out to the back of the house, where the wood fire in the pizza oven crackled happily.

The backyard was Basil's favourite part of the whole place. Large stone flags with buttercups pushing up between them, a large wooden table with mismatched chairs arranged around it, enough for a large party, and warm yellow lights strung overhead, criss crossing back and forth. They weren't on yet of course, the sun wouldn't set for a few hours, but the effect was still pretty. He led the way to the North end of the flagstones and pointed at the sigil etched into it.

Sebastian peered down at it and then up at Basil. "Is that a magic symbol?"

"Yeah, it's for calling the North, when you want to do a big ritual you call all the cardinal directions, it's for protection and for power." Basil said.

"Do your parents do a lot of big rituals?" Sebastian went to one knee to look at the sigil closer. "Is it safe to touch?" He was already reaching a finger towards it.

"Perfectly safe," Dawn said, startling them both. Basil always seemed to forget that his mother moved around without making any kind of sound.

Sebastian gave her a nervous smile, probably because of the startle, and then stroked his finger over the sigil. "It's lovely."

Dawn laughed, pleased. "Thank you dear, it needs redoing every year or so, but it's always come in handy when we need it. Now, both of you come in and choose what you want on your pizzas."

~

DINNER PUT Basil's nerves to rest. The smell of woodsmoke, the delicious cheesy pizzas made fresh, the gentle conversation as Dawn and Russ learned about Sebastian and he made jokes and told stories about the unlikely things he'd seen in his travels, all combined to make a highly pleasant evening.

"And was it really a poltergeist?" Russ asked. He leaned forward, chin propped on his hand, listening raptly to Sebastian's tale.

"I have no idea." Sebastian spread his hands wide. "Nothing showed up on my camera, and although I had all the audio recordings, it wasn't enough to prove anything. And the home owners were sick of waiting for me to solve it, so I had to leave."

"Maybe you two should go back," Russ said. "Basil could try and draw it out."

Basil hurriedly swallowed his mouth of hot mushroom and ham pizza. "Mm, maybe? Where did you say this one was again?"

"Kapiti Coast," Sebastian said, turning towards Basil. The sun was on its way down, and the golden orange light lit up Sebastian's face, accentuating all his features in the best way, catching a sparkle in his eyes. Basil forgot how to breathe. "You know, just up the coast from Wellington?"

"Mm, sounds delightful," Basil murmured.

Dawn's phone started ringing - a Stevie Nicks song - and she sighed and got up from the table, answering it and walking a bit away. "Hello?"

Russ looked between Basil and Sebastian and chuckled. "I'm so glad you two have found each other," he said. "I knew it would happen this year, some time and I was waiting and waiting."

That broke Basil out of his reverie. "Dad, you didn't *do something* did you? A spell or ritual to attract something?"

Russ held up his hands. "Calm down. No, I didn't do anything, I simply asked the cards if there was, you know, anything in store for you this year. In the love department, and they said your true love was on his way."

Basil felt his entire head go red at the words 'true love'.

"Dad, it's only been a couple of months," he muttered, setting his pizza down so he could cover his face with both hands.

He felt Sebastian's cool hand on his and let him pry his hands off his face. Sebastian kissed him softly. "I think it's sweet." Then he turned to look at Russ again. "Did the cards like, tell you what I'm like or?"

"A young man with dark hair," Russ said. His smile broadened. "And a willingness to accept the supernatural."

"That's me," Sebastian said, sounding pleased. He squeezed Basil's hands. "It's fine, I think it's sweet, really."

Basil remembered that Sebastian's parents were largely hands off in their dealings with him, giving him money and then leaving him to it. He was suddenly glad that Russ and Dawn cared so much about him that they'd do readings about his happiness.

"You what?!" Dawn's voice got suddenly louder and all three men at the table looked over at her. "You can't have, they can't have... a what? An entity?"

Sebastian's eyes went wider and he perked up like a puppy who'd heard the rattle of a kibble bag. "What did she just say?"

Russ frowned. "Dawn?"

Dawn smothered the lower half of her mobile phone with her hand and peered at them. "The yarn bombers have discovered something. Or possibly summoned it, it's not clear. They were putting together some kind of art work on the outskirts of the reserve and then... something happened."

Sebastian was out of his seat in flash, his own phone out. "Where are they? I can help."

Basil got up slightly slower. "Are you sure that's a good idea?"

His question was drowned by Dawn who spoke into the phone again. "Basil and his boyfriend are going to come in our car, they'll sort it out."

"We didn't exactly agree," Basil murmured, but it was to himself. He knew no force in the universe could keep Sebastian away from a mystical mystery and Basil knew his way around the island and his parent's dodgy old car.

"Yes, he's a supernatural investigator on the Youtubes," Dawn said, and Basil cringed again.

"Keys are in the bowl by the door," Russ said, helping himself to the last of Basil's pizza. "Call if you need back up."

Sebastian had vanished back into the house, no doubt to collect up his camera gear. Basil got the details of where the yarn bombers had been, and then followed, feeling the happy butter-flies in his stomach roiling into nervousness.

"Do you want me to drive?" Sebastian asked, as they went down the path to the car. "I know you don't usually, around Auckland."

"No, uh, the car is temperamental, and very old. If you don't know the tricks it won't go." Basil said. "Besides, I know where we're going."

"Right, thank you then," Sebastian got into the passenger seat with all his camera gear on his lap, and immediately began to pull out his GoPro and set it up. Basil got the car started, turned down the blaring National Radio programme off the radio and started to drive.

The drive to the forest reserve was barely ten minutes, the roads largely empty and Basil being familiar with the route.

It was quite dark by this stage of the evening. Basil pulled into the small carpark alongside a few other cars which must have belonged to the yarn bombers.

"Mum said they were on the outskirts," Basil said, uncertainly.

"We should be able to see flashlights or hear them," Sebastian said. "Once we get out of the car, I mean."

Basil smiled at him in the dim light, feeling his enthusiasm and excitement and letting those energies flow into him as well. He hadn't expected this kind of Christmas gift for Sebastian, but here they were.

"How much are you loving this?" Basil asked. Sebastian's teeth flashed white as he grinned.

"So much. Come on, let's go find them."

They got out of the car, and having slammed his door shut, Basil pulled out his own phone and put it on 'torch' mode. A shadowy figure emerged from the path and cleared its throat.

Basil had been about to throw his hands up and cast a shield, but the clearing throat stopped him. Ghosts and monsters probably didn't go around clearing their throats, right?

"Hello? Are you Basil?" The shape said. It sounded very human, and vaguely familiar.

"Is that Sue?" Basil replied.

Sebastian got his nightlight working and the area was bathed in a soft white glow. Marjorie's daughter Sue stood before them, looking concerned.

"Yes, it's me."

"This is Sebastian," Basil said, quickly, because Sebastian was already approaching her and probably about to launch into presenter mode.

"Hello," Sue said. She was squinting a little in the light.

"Do you mind if I film this? I have a show online, where I hunt ghosts and things."

Sue shrugged. "Sure why not, if you can get rid of the thing is really what I'm most concerned about."

"So, what happened?" Sebastian asked.

"Well, we were setting up a new display, uh, covers for the bench seats at the rest area, and a couple of pieces which wrap around the nearby trees. They were going to be a Christmas surprise, but once we had them all arranged, this thing appeared and cursed us out."

Basil's heart sped up at those words. What could it be? Some kind of demonic entity? An angry spirit?

"Did you get a good look at it?" Sebastian said, barely containing his excitement.

"Well, yeah, and you can too, it's hanging around. Come on, they're all down here."

"You didn't run from it?" Sebastian glanced at Basil, who shrugged, as surprised as he was.

"Nah, I mean, it's not like it attacked. It just swore a lot," Sue said. She turned on her heels and led the way down the path through the trees.

IT WAS VERY QUIET, the stars quickly being hidden by the canopy as they walked into the native forest. Sebastian lapsed into silence, filming as they walked behind Sue. The only sounds their footsteps and the occasional rustle of something in the under-brush. It was a hot night, but under the trees it became cooler. Basil kept his eyes on the path, afraid of tripping and falling and being on Sebastian's show again as the witch who fell down.

A thought occurred to him then, about why Sue had called his mother in the first place. Why his mother? He'd thought that as far as everyone knew, Dawn and Russ were just retired hippies, like most of the population of Surfdale seemed to be.

"Uh, Sue?" he said, feeling terribly obvious to be breaking the silence to talk.

"Mm?"

"What uh, what were you expecting when you called Dawn about this?"

"Oh, I thought she'd come down and help us out, I forgot you were staying," Sue said, lightly.

"Help out..." Basil said, softly. "Do you mean...?" he wasn't sure how to finish the sentence. He had no idea how much she knew after all.

"Yeah, do a spell and set it to rest maybe," Sue said. "I mean, a few of the yarn bombers have traces of magic, but nothing like Dawn. I guess she thinks you've inherited her powers and can handle it okay?"

Basil stopped walking for a moment. Sebastian, who had been a step behind, put his hand on his lower back and the warmth reassured Basil enough to keep going. "So uh, I suppose you all know about... uh, witchcraft then?"

"Oh, didn't you know that we knew?" Sue stopped and turned to look at her, stricken. "I didn't think she'd have sent you if you didn't, Marjorie said -" she cut herself off and shook her head. "I'm sorry, I think, uh, I stepped in it there. We're meant to pretend we don't know, aren't we?"

"Meant to pretend?" Basil echoed back.

She shook her head. "Let's get this thing sorted out and then we can talk about the community, shall we?"

Basil's stomach turned over unpleasantly but she was right, they needed to focus on the matter at hand.

Sue turned a corner and when they followed the path opened up to a small rest area, with three park benches. These were decorated with knitted patterns, something about which tugged at Basil's memory. The area was crowded with ten people, most of them looking concerned, or worried rather than terrified.

Sebastian inhaled sharply and Basil looked at him and then at what he was pointing his camera at. The tenth figure, which Basil had barely glanced at before his attention went to the benches and the knitted patterns, was not human. It looked human-ish, with two legs and a head and all the facial features in the right place, but it wasn't human.

"And this is the uh, being you... found?"

"They didn't find me," the being said. The voice was rough and gravelly, but Basil didn't get a masculine feeling off of it. "They woke me up and now they don't know what to do."

Sebastian and Basil exchanged looks, looks which said 'well which of us is going to go talk to it?'. Sebastian gave a slight nod, Basil swallowed his fear and approached the being.

"My apologies, kind sir, er, ma'- ... uh, folk? I uh, well, I'm here to help out however I can. Would you like to explain what you were doing before they, uh, woke you?"

"Sleeping in my tree," the thing said. "And you can call me Leaf."

"Leaf, hello, I'm Basil and this is Sebastian, he's recording this if that's all right with you?"

"Recording?" Leaf peered at Sebastian and scowled. "I want to go back to sleep."

"Right, we'd like to help you do that too."

Leaf paced back and forth, clearing the path of knitters, and Basil saw green things sprouting from where they had tread.

Leaf, was sleeping, new plants where they've walked... right, I think I know.

Basil half turned towards Sebastian and spoke to him, pretending as hard as he could that he wasn't speaking to the camera. "I think they're some kind of tree spirit, and I think the problem is the pattern the knitters used."

Sue moved to beside Basil and frowned. "What's wrong with the pattern we used?"

"Well, I can't be sure," Basil said. "But they might be magic symbols."

"Of course they're fucking magic symbols," Leaf exclaimed. "You don't just wake people up with ordinary knitting do you?"

"Well, we did today!" One of the younger knitters piped up with. Leaf fixed them with a glare.

"Let me, uh, let me see the knitting more closely, I suppose," Basil said. "Can we get some light on what you've done?"

The knitting circle moved in, all turned their lights and phones onto the knitting on the benches and Basil squatted down to examine them.

"What do you think, Basil?" Sebastian prompted. "Are they sigils you've seen before?"

"They did sort of bug me when we first came in," Basil said. "But I haven't studied them myself."

"Where did you find this pattern, Ana?" One of them said, with a trace of snippiness.

"It was a free pattern online," Ana said, with a trace of defensiveness. "It was like, Celtic or something."

Basil sniffed. "I don't think it's Celtic so much as it's Druidic." He traced his fingers over the edge of one particular symbol which wasn't at all unlike a summoning sigil he'd used once before. "In which case the way you placed them all, and then the bit on the tree..." he looked around, managed a smile for the camera. "You summoned the tree spirit. But it's all right, we just have to unravel a corner of each of the symbols and they should be able to go back to sleep."

"About damn time," Leaf grumbled.

Sebastian asked a couple more questions as the knitters got to work, two of them taking each piece of knitting and unravelling the stitches. Basil helped with the main summoning one, which was arranged artfully on the seat of a bench.

In order to ensure it worked perfectly, he summoned up his magical power, and extended his senses out, tracking the feeling of the inadvertent spell being dismantled, and monitoring the energy of the tree spirit.

As the last stitch was undone he felt a sort of relief, a tension he'd barely been aware of when he'd walked into the area released. He stood up straight and went over to Leaf. A tree spirit was practically one of the fey, and although they had done their part to let them return to sleep, politeness was never wasted.

"I am terribly sorry for the disturbance, Leaf. And the Waiheke yarn bombers are all sorry as well. Aren't you?" He used a slightly severe tone for that last bit, and the knitters all murmured that yes, they were sorry and they wouldn't do it again.

Leaf stared around all of them severely and then nodded. "Very well. See that you don't!" Then they turned and walked directly into the trunk of the tree, sparkling around the edges as they vanished.

The knitters were silent for a moment and then broke into soft and very tentative applause.

"That was wonderful, thank you Basil," Sue said. She shook his hand warmly.

"Yes, well, not much to it really," he said. "Just, perhaps, don't use knitting patterns you find online in the future?"

There was laughter and someone said "Uh, that's where all the best patterns are," and Basil's heart sank.

"We promise not to use any symbols without researching them first," Ana said, earnestly.

That seemed like the best they could offer.

DAWN AND RUSS were waiting at home with a large bowl of fruit salad, home made meringues and whipped cream. They sat at the table out the back and ate and drank white wine, and Sebastian regaled them with the whole story.

"It's going to make a great episode," he said, finally and kissed Basil on the cheek. He smelled of kiwifruit and whipped cream. Basil flushed happily. "I'll need to film some intro and outro stuff, and maybe some scene setting things around the island, but yeah. Will be a really good one."

"And you're all right with that, Basil?" Russ asked, his expression a little concerned. "Being on camera while magic things happen?"

Basil took Sebastian's hand and squeezed it. "Yeah, I mean, I probably won't watch the episode or read the comments, but yeah. It's all right."

"I'm proud of you," Sebastian said, softly.

Dawn and Russ both smiled wider. "So are we, son," Dawn said. "And that's a relief, we won't have to be quite so guarded at the party tomorrow."

"Guarded?" Basil said, tilting his head to one side.

"Oh well, uh, everyone on the island knows we're witches," Russ said. "But we knew you were a bit shy about it, so we asked people to pretend they didn't know, so you could be comfortable."

"But... you must've..." Basil sighed and tried to remember when he was a teenager, it had felt like they'd had a few more witchy friends back then. It was only once he'd moved away that he'd assumed his parents had gone more into the broom closet. But instead they'd done it for him, and there he'd avoided coming to visit them, even though they were just being who they are. "I'm so sorry, I didn't ever want you to pretend to be something you're not," he said finally.

"Oh, only when you're around," Dawn said. "We hated to see you so awkward, that's all. But now you're really coming out of your shell, and I believe we have Sebastian to thank for that."

All three of them smiled at Sebastian who had helped himself to another meringue with cream. He grinned. "No problem."

"Right, well, big day tomorrow," Russ said. "Christmas Eve, so we'll have our big Midsummer solstice party, people will be turning up from midday and there's lots of cooking to do."

Dawn offered the bowl of meringues to Sebastian and he took another. "Thank you."

"My pleasure. Sleep well you two, Russ put a nice strong sound reduction charm on the walls so don't worry about waking us up."

Basil hid his head in his hands. "Mum!"

Once their footsteps had retreated, Sebastian slipped his arms around Basil and nuzzled his neck. "Your parents are really lovely."

Basil dropped his hands to the table and sighed. "But they're so embarrassing."

"But they love you," Sebastian said. "And so do I."

Basil kissed him softly on the mouth. "I love you, too. Do you want to stay out for a while longer, or go to bed?"

"I think we could stay out a little longer," Sebastian said. "Give me a chance to charm you with my knowledge of constellations. I bet you can see a ton of them out here."

Basil got up to switch off the fairy lights in the backyard, took Sebastian's hand and led him to the grassy bank at the back of the section. There they sat down, arms around each other, and looked at the stars.

Christmas was never entirely an easy time, but it was good to be around people who loved him, and more than that, accepted him for who he was, awkward or not.

15

A SUMMON, A HOWL

Danny had everything lined up perfectly. He had all his tools before him - a magical mise en place.

He had chosen the woods because of the *trespassers will be shot* sign.

Danny wasn't worried about the sign. Someone like him, a skinny college kid not remarkable in any way, simply average, could get away with things purely by being so easily ignored.

Well, after tonight he wouldn't be overlooked.

He glanced upwards, confirming once again that the stars were in the correct position.

Danny triple checked the runes he'd copied from the grimoire and placed them on the leafy floor of the forest.

He took a deep, centring breath.

Now to say the words.

Danny took a moment to clear his throat. The grimoire was clear that ill-placed coughs or stutters would ruin the spell.

The results of an ill-delivered spell were heinous.

He hitched up his jeans and began.

"O, holy lord of darkness, child of the moon, destroyer of the light, called Mongrel of the Forest and Insidious Darkling, hear me now. I address you as a master of the midnight arts, I bid you listen and obey my will. Come to this place now!"

He crouched, picked up the dried bones he had gathered in the desert and scattered them in the centre of the spell circle.

"I conjure you with bones scavenged in the midday sun and with whiskey distilled from a fairy's tears." He poured the dram out over the nearest of the bones. He'd used the last of his savings for that tiny bottle of whiskey.

He picked up the third thing, a choke chain, the kind used with particularly large dogs. "I conjure you with my will and with this spell I bind you."

Danny waited, not daring to breathe as the nearby trees creaked and bent, as the air in the centre of the circle shimmered and coalesced into golden light. The light rippled, and Danny's body rebelled against the sight. His head hurt like there were daggers behind his eyes.

He closed his eyes, focused on his breathing, opened his eyes and tossed the chain the instant he saw a form.

The Mongrel of the Forest growled as the chain settled about its neck. It looked similar to a werewolf from an old Hammer horror.

Misshapen limbs, arms far too long, head smaller than expected on broad shoulders. Hairy with fangs in a scarred muzzle.

"You dare? Bind me?" The Forest Mongrel growled, and stood taller, the hairs on its back - or were they bristles? - standing up and giving it an even more monstrous appearance.

"Yes, I dare!" Danny's heart thundered but he knew that he had to project confidence or the beast would find a way to escape.

The Mongrel huffed, its breath wafted to Danny's nose, fetid as old meat. "To what purpose?"

This was the moment, the one Danny had worked so long for.

"I demand you give me a piece of your power."

The Mongrel moved closer, testing the boundaries of the ward to lean in and peer into Danny's eyes.

Danny didn't waver, although his heart pounded and his instincts insisted that he run.

"Why?" it snarled.

"Because I have you bound here," Danny said. "If you do not give me what I demand I will destroy you where you stand. Is that the fate you desire?"

"The fate I desire..." The Mongrel shuddered, hunched forward and made a wheezing sound. Was it laughing?

The Mongrel straightened its back again. "Idiot. The forest is my fate. Tell me what you will give me. Freedom is guaranteed if we bargain. Ancient rules."

Danny remembered now, the book had mentioned exchanges.

"I offer the color of my hair," he said. His hair was mouse brown, as average as the rest of him. If the Mongrel took the color he'd have interesting silver or white hair.

"Not a fae," the Mongrel snorted. "Don't want that. Want a year of your life."

This, too, was familiar. Danny had read of these bargains. One year at the end of his life wasn't too much to ask. He'd be old by then..

"Very well." Danny nodded and held out his hand as if to shake. "One year of my life."

The Mongrel's eyes flickered with fire that wasn't present in the forest. The words of the grimoire swam in his memory.

Soon he would be a powerful warlock. He would get people's attention - in classes, at parties. He'd land a gorgeous partner and live the life he dreamed of.

The Mongrel extended a claw.

They shook - hand to claw, sealing the bargain.

"I will take your year now."

"No, a year at the end of my-"

"Didn't specify," The Mongrel said. Its claws wrapped tight around Danny's wrist and tugged him closer. "My choice."

"Oh fuck." Danny said. "Then give me your power, as agreed."

"Didn't say which piece..." The Mongrel grinned, its fangs sharp, filling its mouth. It leaned in, opening its mouth wide.

The transfer took mere seconds. One moment Danny's head was in the beast's mouth, the next, he was the beast.

The Mongrel, now inside of Danny's body, stepped back, straightened the collar on his shirt and smiled a perfectly average human smile. He held himself better than Danny usually did.

By contrast, Danny's back hurt, the stoop that the Mongrel had was an affliction, and it ached.

He wanted to move, to grab at Danny, to snatch, but he was overwhelmed with strange new instincts. His limbs didn't respond. The chain around his neck burned, and he scrabbled at it, trying to get it off.

"I'll see you back here, in one year," Mongrel-in-Danny said. "Thanks for the bargain."

"Wait, stop," Danny tried to say, but the muzzle wasn't familiar, and the fangs inhibited the movement of the tongue.

Mongrel-in-Danny smirked, saluted, and walked into the night with a bounce in its step.

Danny-in-Mongrel threw his head back and howled his frustration into the forest night.

16

ONE MAN HIDE AND SEEK

"You don't have to do this, you know," Val said, her dark eyes wide.

Cass had returned to help with the first steps. Cass shook her head, pulled the last of the stuffing out of the doll and wiggled the fabric husk at Val. Val batted her hand away, eyes wide, frowning.

"Yeah, I do. If I don't go through with it everyone will say I'm a coward."

"You mean Jack will."

"I'm not a coward," Cass said, as if Val hadn't spoken.

"But this is the real thing," Val's teasing tone was gone. She put her hand on Cass's. "One Man Hide and Seek really works. I know it does."

"You've never done it."

"I saw it online."

"Sure, if it's on the internet it must be true."

"Seriously, there were people's experiences. And not just like, stories, there's creepy photos and video. You saw the one with the shadow. It was eerie."

"That stuff can all be faked."

"I couldn't see how it was fake. Besides, the instructions for this came from Japan and they have the scariest ghost movies."

"It won't work because there's no such thing as ghosts."

Cass pulled her hand back from under Val's and picked up a plastic funnel. She filled doll with rice. The first part of the ritual was craft, household items and weirdness. Cass picked up her phone to check the next step. It said you were supposed to put fingernail clippings into the doll, along with the rice. Cass had just redone her nail polish that morning so she took off her socks and cut her toenails. That would do.

You were meant to use red thread when you sewed the doll up, to symbolise blood or surgery or something. She'd looked for red thread but there was none in the house, so she sewed the doll's back closed with orange embroidery floss. The instructions went on and on about salt and its protective powers. Val searched the kitchen and found a jar of iodised table salt at the back of the pantry. Cass put it in her hiding place.

PREPARATION DONE, she sent Val home. Val's face was pale, her hands fluttered like an old lady's, worrying.

"You don't have to go through with it, you really don't!"

"Yes I really do, now go."

"Promise you'll call if it goes wrong?"

"Promise. Check that no one's hanging around outside to rustle the branches, scratch the windows or knock on the door, would you?"

"Okay. But you don't-"

Cass closed the door on Val.

YOU STARTED the game by naming the doll and submerging it in water in the bath.

Cass called hers 'Dolly', she couldn't be bothered thinking up something clever. Their house didn't have a bath, so she used the bathroom sink. Approximations would be fine. She said the words right though, took a nail file and stabbed the doll three times just like the instructions said.

SHE WAITED.

SHE RETREATED TO HER 'HIDING PLACE' then, her safe space. Val had helped make a fort under the dining table. She had a view of the TV which apparently would show if ghosts were around. She sat, making a nest out of the cushions and watched old movies for 20 minutes.

SHE'D DOZED off when the picture flickered. The TV had been playing an old black and white horror movie, because Cass thought it was ironic. The picture flickered twice more and died but she could still hear the soundtrack crackling through the surround sound. Cass tried changing channels with the remote, hitting the power button, switching inputs, nothing worked. She crawled across to the socket and unplugged the television. Sound continued to sound from the speakers. Her arms prickled with goosebumps.

SHE GOT up to check on the doll.

THE SINK SAT EMPTY. No doll, no water, no plug. All her hairs stood on end.

. . .

No one could have moved it. Her parents were out of town. Her friends were safe at home. The doll had gone.

Hiding, just like it was supposed to. Cass had to find it and end the game. Simple. How far could a doll hardly bigger than her hand get? Even if it did have a ghost in it?

Cass tiptoed around the house, her heart pounding. What had possessed her to do this? How much of an idiot was she? Had she endangered her life to impress her crush? Why had she signed up to do this thing straight out of a horror movie?

She stepped into the dining room, flashlight on and looked under the table. She ran her hand along the seats of the chairs. Nothing. She opened the drawers of the sideboard. Found napkins, placemats, fancy bottles of whiskey.

The doll wasn't there. She searched the house again, more thoroughly. How long since she'd started the ritual? It felt like hours.

A noise across the room, over by the door. She spun, stabbing the dark with the beam of the flashlight. Nothing there. Her heart beat so hard she was surprised it didn't hurt.

Cass closed the door to the dining room firmly. She crossed the hallway to her bedroom.

She was angry at herself for not taking this seriously to start with.

"I'm an idiot. I'm one of those dumb teenagers in a horror movie who play at summoning demons. I should've taken this seriously."

. . .

SHE SHOULD HAVE PUT lines of salt in front of these doors like the website had warned her to. The doll could be anywhere by now.

CASS TOOK a deep breath before entering her room, tried to get a handle on her fear.

"DOLLY, ARE YOU IN HERE?"

INSIDE, things had been moved. Mr Boo, her soft toy elephant, was balanced upside down on a lamp. Her diary lay open on the bed. She reached over to close it. She'd left it in her drawer, in the bedside table, safe and secret.

It was open on one of her unsent letters to Jack. Her face flushed red, her fear retreated and she lost her temper instead.

"I'M NOT PLAYING AROUND ANYMORE. This game is over! Come on out!" Cass's voice sounded strange, cracked and high. She shone her flashlight around the room. Her stomach dropped.

There was writing on the mirror above her chest of drawers.

CASS FUMBLED IN HER POCKET, her hands were shaking so badly she almost dropped her phone. She took several photos, worried that the shaking would ruin the image. She flicked to burst mode and held down the button.

Something, she presumed the doll, had used one of her lipsticks to spell out 'Play with me'. She screwed up her eyes and swallowed a lump in her throat.

. . .

THAT AFTERNOON she'd been sitting with her friends in the front room. They drank beers filched from Jack's Dad and stared out the window at the rain. It had rained on and off all day, ruining their plans to hit the skate park. Somehow, they'd got to talking about weird stuff. Supernatural stuff. Val started in on this ghost summoning ritual she'd read about online. Val knew about lots of kooky crap.

"Don't be ridiculous," Cass had said. The beer made her loud, braver than usual. "There's no such thing as ghosts."

"How do you know?" Val asked.

"Yeah, my aunt once had a séance when she was like, our age," Jack said. "And the cups in the kitchen rattled all at once and there wasn't an earthquake or anything." Cass looked at Jack, who turned to her. Cass wanted to keep her attention, even if she could feel her cheeks getting warm.

"I just know is all," Cass said. "There's no proof."

"How can you be so sure?" Val had said. "There's no proof that gravity exists but everyone believes in that."

"Duh, gravity is totally provable," Cass said.

Matt demonstrated by dropping an empty beer bottle on the ground.

Val rolled her eyes.

"So, if you're so sure there's no such thing as ghosts..." Matt had said.

"I'm sure," Cass said.

"We should try it out, do a séance or something. I'm totally bored," Matt said.

"Yeah, or Cass could try that ritual you found, Val," Jack said. Her eyes were still on Cass, daring her to argue. Her eyes were dreamy, grey and bright.

"Sure whatever," Cass said, her heart racing. "I don't care, I'll do it."

Matt whooped and clapped his hands together.

"This is going to be awesome!"

"But I'll do it alone, okay? I don't want any of you sticking ice down my back, jumping out at me from behind a door or some cheap trick like that." Her heart thudded as she looked defiantly back at the group.

"Don't be ridiculous," Val had tried to make peace. "One Man Hide and Seek is real, it's dangerous magic. We shouldn't be messing with it."

"Magic and ghosts, it sounds real dangerous," Jack said, laughing. It spurred Cass on.

"I'm doing it, tonight." Cass watched Jack's eyes soften, her sneer turning into a smile. Was she impressed? Cass thought she looked impressed.

Jack lingered after the others left, her hands stuck deep in the pockets of her cargo pants.

"Listen, take care tonight alright?" she said. Her eyebrows raised up her forehead, earnestly. Cass hoped that she'd stayed to talk because she cared, just a bit.

"Of course I will," Cass had replied. It was the wrong response, because she sounded too tough, almost like she was mocking her. But Cass didn't feel weak or scared, so why should she act like it?

"Sure," Jack had said. She turned on her heel, but slowly. Was she giving Cass space to say something else?

"I'll tell you everything," Cass said, surprising herself. Jack fixed her with a stare over her shoulder. What had she just offered? "I mean, about tonight. I'll tell you how it goes."

"Cool." She'd smiled then, and Cass's heart generated serious electricity.

IN THE DARKNESS, Cass chewed her nails down to painful stubs. She'd been through most of the rooms in the house, chewing. The only rooms she hadn't searched were her big brother's room and the bathroom, and she didn't think it would be in there. She really wanted to turn the lights on but the instructions had been specific about keeping the house dark. She'd learned enough to trust the instructions.

HER BROTHER'S room was almost empty. He'd moved out a week ago and there were just a few leftover boxes where his stuff used to be stacked up against the stripped bed. Cass lay down on the floor and checked under it. She hoped nothing would jump out at her. While she was peering, squinting in the dark, she heard a noise from inside one of the boxes. A movement. Hopefully it was just a rat.

SHE BIT HER LIP. She had it cornered. Trapped in a box. She stood and looked at the boxes. There was one on top of the stack that hadn't been sealed. Her heart beat double time as she reached towards the flap on top of the box.

SHE YANKED the flap back and something leapt out.

Cass stepped back, gasping.

It was on the floor before she could grab it. It ran between her legs and away. Cass swung around and her flashlight caught a glimpse of the doll running away into the hall.

Cass swallowed, she knew she couldn't waste time on fear. Her legs didn't want to move though.

"Come on, legs." She thought of Jack's face. Took a deep breath and ran after the doll. It pushed into a cupboard; its tiny, rounded mitten hands were surprisingly nimble with the edge of the door.

"No, you don't," Cass said through gritted teeth. She leapt, slid down the hall rug like it was the softball pitch and seized the doll with both hands. The impact winded her and she nearly lost her grip.

The doll squirmed, trying to free itself. She squeezed it hard and lay still for a moment, getting her breath back. It started making a horrible keening noise.

"Skreeeeeeeeeeeeeee!"

"Quiet!" Cass shouted. The doll squirmed in her hands, trying to get free. "I've caught you! I've won! The game is over!" The doll kept squirming. What had she done wrong? She wondered. It was hide and seek right? You caught the other person and then the game was over. But the doll still had something in it.

Clutching the doll in one hand she went back to her laptop and checked the instructions. Salt water. She was supposed to spit on the doll and then soak it in salt water. Kitchen sink. She curled her hand into her chest, pressing the doll against her skin to stop it getting away. The keening noise stopped, which was a relief. It was easier to think without that noise.

She found the half empty jar of salt and ran the cold water, topping the jar up. The doll wasn't moving any more. It must have guessed the game was over. Her chest was cold though, aching where the doll was pressed against her shirt, squirming. She swilled the jar around, mixing the salt through, lifted it to her lips. There was a powerful jolt from the doll, water slopped down Cass's arm and she stumbled back into the cupboards.

The doll squirmed and made the noise again and Cass saw a huge shadow in the darkness. A ragged spectral image, all teeth and softly glowing sockets where the eyes should be. It was impossibly large, looming up to the ceiling, spreading to the corners of the room. Her chest ached.

For a moment she didn't breathe. Then she shook her head once, and glared at the thing.

"No. This is over,' Cass said through clenched teeth. She tried to move the doll to the sink but her arm had seized up. The ache in her chest was severe, she was finding it hard to take a full lungful of air. An asthma attack?

Cass sucked in what air she could, tears leaked out of her eyes from fear and frustration. She sipped some water and slowly poured it over her other hand, soaking the doll. It went limp.

Cass flexed her fingers and drew the doll away from her. Her arm muscles screamed with the effort. She carefully put it into the kitchen sink and leaned forward. The salt flavour was overwhelming. She vomited it out onto the doll.

Nothing happened. Cass stared down at the plastic bead eyes and shouted as loud as she could.

"I win! I win! I win!" It lay lifeless in her hand, just a doll. Cass gripped the kitchen counter with both hand as her legs were threatening to give out. She flipped on the light. She was surprised the kitchen looked normal.

She took the lid off the slow cooker, pulled out the heavy ceramic bowl and placed it, bottom down, on top of the doll. She'd burn the wretched thing in daylight.

Cass met up with the others at the skatepark in the morning. She'd been pleased that the sun rose that day, and especially pleased that it was warm. She felt cold all over and she'd been shivering on the walk over. Her friends looked expectant. She took her time telling them what had happened, spinning the story for dramatic effect. She showed them the photos, but the ones of the doll moving had come out too dark. They said she'd written the lipstick words. It's so easy to fake images.

There was nothing conclusive. She put the smouldering remains of the doll out for them to look at. She planned to bury it far, far away from her house. Val refused to touch it, but Matt picked it up, mimed making it walk.

"That's not funny," Val snapped. "You shouldn't be touching it."

"Fine, whatever," Matt said, he looked hurt. "Let's just bury the damn thing then."

"Yes, please," Cass said. Matt and Val took the doll over into the bushes and started digging. Cass looked over at Jack.

"Seriously, nothing happened last night did it?" Jack said.

"Yeah, it did," Cass said, smiling in what she hoped was a mysterious and knowing way.

"You just freaked yourself out and didn't sleep."

"Look, I have one more thing to show you, but you have to promise that you won't freak out," Cass said. Jack smiled, a silent promise.

Slowly, drawing out the suspense, and trying to stop herself from hyperventilating, Cass unbuttoned her check shirt. Gingerly, she pulled her t-shirt down and exposed the skin that the doll had been pressed against. Her chest was marked with the blackened, burnt image of a face. It wasn't a hideous demon or a skull, just a simple face. Like a child's drawing, with big black pits for eyes and a wide, toothy smile. The skin around it was red and raw. She'd spent several hours that morning scrubbing at it with a facecloth, then a loofah, then salt, anything she could think of. The face had remained the same, like she'd been branded. It made her very nervous, but then so did being this close to Jack.

Jack very slowly reached her hand out towards her.

"Is it okay if I touch it?"

"Sure."

Cass's breath quickened as she watched her fingertips brush gently over her skin. She looked up at her and with awe but she thought there was some fear in her eyes as well.

"What happened to you?" she asked, her voice low, almost reverent.

Cass felt a shudder down her spine. She looked over to where the others had put the doll into the Earth.

That'd be it right? All she had to do. Her chest ached where the face was imprinted, and she buttoned her shirt back up.

"Why don't you come over tonight?" Cass asked, one hand moving to push her hair behind her ear, suddenly sure of what she wanted.

"Your parents still away?"

"Uh huh. Come over tonight and we can try it again."

"Try what?"

"Hide and seek."

BLIND DATE

I sat in the café window so I'd be obvious, easily spotted. I held the coffee cup in both hands, curling my fingers around the cup for warmth. My gloves meant I couldn't hold it with one hand, woollen fingerless gloves are tricky that way, but I liked the hotness on my hands anyway. The night was bitter and rainy and I was pleased to be inside.

My stomach turned over when the door opened, I hadn't thought I would be this nervous but then I didn't go on a lot of blind dates. I had this image in my head of what it would be like when he finally turned up, our eyes would meet from across the room and he'd come over, sit down and just start talking. We'd have so much in common, we'd be able to talk about everything. I love classic novels and in my mind he would be carrying a copy of *Dracula*. Corny, I know, and actually totally inappropriate but in my head it was super romantic that he had it. We'd talk for hours, he'd order cake for us to share, we'd laugh about stuff. He would be so attractive, pale skin like so pale he was almost translucent. He would have an edge of danger about him, a mystique. He'd be so sexy, talking in a low gravelly voice, a voice that betrayed his years of dark experiences.

We would talk about blood, of course. It was inevitable that the talk would eventually turn to blood, his, mine. Drinking it. His handle on the website had been 'O-positivelover' after all.

I put my coffee down as the door opened again and he walked in. He was wearing a black suit jacket with a white camellia in the pocket – the signal. It was really him. He wasn't pale, his cheeks were rosy from the cold and his eyes were normal, just brown. He sat down opposite me, looking nervous rather than self-assured. He held a beat-up copy of *Dracula* stacked with an even older-looking copy of *Carmilla*. I could smell the fear, he was sweating with it.

I smiled to put him at ease, I let my fangs show between my lips. He wasn't the dream man I'd imagined, but his blood would taste sweet all the same.

18

ROOM SERVICE

Hotel towels aren't big enough, Mabel thought. They're standard towel size rather than the generous bath sheets she used at home. But hotel towels, white, scratchy, bleached, washed hundreds of times had an advantage. Unlike the plush, Egyptian cotton at home, hotel towels are very absorbent. You only have to wipe your leg once with a hotel towel and it's dry. It can dry your entire body no problem at all and still have patches which are completely dry. Something about the number of washes, maybe, or the detergent they use on them.

Whatever it was, Mabel was thankful for the absorbent nature of hotel towels on this day. There was so much blood on the white shiny tiles of the bathroom floor. So much to clean up. So much evidence to remove. All four of the hotel bath towels and the two hand driers were being utilised.

She hadn't even meant to do it. Well, no that wasn't quite right. She'd meant to do it, but she hadn't planned to.

Not yet.

Not like that anyway.

In fact, she'd been toying with the idea of never again. Just giving up altogether, but he'd pushed her. He'd wanted it. Been all touchy and pushy. Oh, he hadn't said anything out loud, but they never did. They implied it, teasing her with their body language.

She sighed as she scrubbed at the underside of the bathroom sink, the blood did spatter everywhere. It wouldn't do to leave a single drop in this room. Couldn't have them connecting her to the body.

The sun had been going down outside the window, twenty third floor. The light was weirdly orange inside the room.

"What do you want?" She'd asked from the kitchen area. She'd waved two bottles, a white wine and an expensive mineral water laced with exotic fruit.

"Whatever you're having," he'd said. She'd poured two wines and joined him on the hard hotel couch. She'd really been trying to give it up, but it was difficult not to think about it. His breath came noisily out of his nose, setting her teeth on edge.

"Shall we watch a movie?" She made her voice bright, trying to distract herself from his twitching fingers. From the way his hair smelled. From the knives she could see neatly stacked in their block on the kitchen counter.

"I'm not in the mood for a movie," Ben had said. He'd turned to her, smiling. There was spinach between his left canine and the next tooth over. He'd taken her wine glass and set it on the table. "I've got something else in mind."

It wasn't the sex that made her do it. Mabel could have sex with no problems at all, with the right men she never even considered it. She wasn't one of those tacky Black Widow killers. It was more to do with the way men acted with her. They were so confused about how to be. Trying to appear super sensitive when really they were using every possible opportunity to look at your breasts. They used poetry and romantic comedies and politics to win your trust, making you think that they were intelligent. Then they sat on the couch farting and ignoring all the housework that needed to be done. It got on her nerves.

The only thing she'd found that relieved her stress completely was the killing. She knew it was wrong, and she did feel guilty about it for a day or so after, but there it was. They were always so surprised. That was the thing that really sealed it, the look in their eyes as she overpowered them. That was the reason she had to keep doing it. The disbelief that such as small, mousy woman could be so quick, so handy with a knife. If they didn't look so astounded that a mere woman could unseat them as rulers of the universe she might never do it again.

In the hallway she bundled the dirty towels into the anonymous laundry chute. Letting it join all the other linen in this 800 + room hotel. She stalked the floors of the hotel until she found a maid at work, vanished into the open door of one the suites. She helped herself to the fresh towels on the housekeeper trolley and went back to her room. When they stop being surprised, she told herself. Then I'll be able to stop too.

19

THE WAY YOU LOOK AT GIRLS

Jordan had been kidnapped by a strip club.

He hadn't even meant to go there. He'd just ducked in to avoid a Hare Krishna guy who was trying to sell copies of the *Bhaghavad Gita* on the street.

Inside, he sat and ordered a beer and watched the stage. The girls smiled at him and danced, and it was a nicer place than he'd expected from the outside. The girls in the water tanks to either side of the stage were unearthly, elegant and beautiful.

In fact, the girls were really talented. Jordan was no expert, but he'd seen his share of ballets, dance groups and so on because his sister loved to dance. The strippers here knew their stuff. They could turn, bend and jump, and their feet never made a sound on the stage.

Good as they were, Jordan always had gotten bored easily. He'd been about to leave when the proprietor of the place sat down at his table and gave him a free drink. Jordan, of course, accepted this.

The next thing he knew he was waking up cuffed to a folding chair with a powerful ache in his head. He had no idea how long he'd been there. The proprietor stepped into the room.

"What's going on?" Jordan had said. His throat was raspy and dry, speaking made him cough.

"There's something about you," the proprietor said. "The way you look at the girls, something about your appreciation. It's lucrative. The girls danced better and the guys in the audience spend more when the girls dance better."

"So what?"

"You're mine now," The Proprietor was an unremarkable looking man, round cheeks, greyish brown hair. But his eyes sparkled black in the half light in a way that didn't make sense. "You will stay and watch the girls."

"You're completely crazy," Jordan said. "I have a job to get back to, people will look for me."

"Don't be ridiculous," The Proprietor gestured dismissively. "No one will find you here."

They kept him cuffed during the day. Usually in the main bar area where he was out of the way of The Proprietor's various other businesses.

In the evenings he was let loose, but he was kept in the bar by two things: the ankle monitor and Angelo. Angelo was the bouncer, and he was roughly the size of a minivan. He had a particular way of looking at Jordan, that made him feel like a geeky 13-year-old again and Angelo was every angry bully.

The nights were strange. Jordan could order whatever he liked from the menu. He could order drinks if he didn't get so drunk he couldn't concentrate on the dancing. He could try and ask people for help if Angelo didn't catch on. No one ever seemed to believe him.

Mostly, he watched the girls. As the weeks passed, he got to know their names and their routines. He was kept from them during the day, in the evenings. Their changing rooms were off-limits, and he understood why.

They always smiled extra wide when they were in front of him. He could see that he did influence them by his gaze, and he thought it had something to do with the way he admired them. He revered them not as sex objects, but as beautiful women, as talented dancers. The thought of having sex with any of them was repulsive to him, because he expected, like him, they weren't here by their own free will.

One night, Cherry came up to him after her routine and sat on his lap. This was something the girls did to get more tips, but they always, always focused on the actual patrons, not Jordan. Jordan had no money.

"Listen, J-baby. We want to help you," Cherry said, her shiny red lips close to his cheek. Her voice barely a breath under the heavy dance music.

"What?" Jordan was confused by the way she smelled. He could detect sweat, cheap perfume and something else. Jordan thought of flowers damp with morning dew.

"I've seen them do this before, use guys like this. Guys like you. You used to write poetry I bet?"

Jordan nodded, perplexed. "What's that got to do with anything?"

"The kind of guy you are. It bugs me that he uses you. The other girls don't think it's fair either. We're gonna help you get away."

"I don't think you can."

"Honey, you've seen me dance, but you have no real idea what I can do. Me and the girls, well, we've got some tricks even you haven't seen yet. Even with all your watching." Cherry's eyes were large, a particular shade of pale blue that was almost purple.

Jordan's breath caught in his throat. She was something else, something in the back of his brain told him to run. As if he could.

"I'm sure you have all sorts of talents, Cherry. I just...you can't play a player. The Proprietor is sharp, you know? The best plan I can think of is to borrow someone's coat and try to blend in with the next stag night that comes through." Jordan hadn't meant to tell her that, it was his best plan, what if she was playing him right now?

Cherry chewed her lip. Her eyes were scanning the room, checking for Angelo's attentive ears. "Stag night, that's good. Trust me, alright? I know how this place works, and I have some friends on the outside that will help, I think. I'll be in touch."

The next night Violet sought him out. Violet, with tumbles of pitch-black hair and delicate features, whose shtick was to act shy and vulnerable. She crawled to the edge of the stage on hands and knees and whispered in his ear.

"Cherry's gone, she left a trap, started it all in motion. We know the plan. Make sure you're ready."

He turned his head to reply but she'd already stood up and danced off. She had got to the part of her act where she let herself really dance, having 'overcome' her shyness. Violet was a beautiful dancer, Jordan suspected ballet training in her past. She had a grace and elegance that shone on stage.

The next night Jordan was surrounded by a raucous stag party. One of them had mentioned that he'd seen Jordan there before, and Jordan agreed that he probably had.

The drunken men all raised their eyebrows and nudged each other. The stag party engulfed him and plied him with drinks.

Jordan ordered steaks for everyone at some point in the evening. The beers had gone to his head, and it seemed like the laddish thing to do. While they were all devouring the garlic butter coated rib eyes one of the stag night men, a young one, leaned over to him.

"Tonight's the night, wait for the signal."

Jordan nodded as if he didn't care and chewed on his steak. On stage Valeria and Rose were doing a mirror-theme dance. The club was packed, which was unusual for a Tuesday.

Jordan turned to see who was in the tanks tonight. He saw Lily's trademark purple hair and Cissy's blonde curls, spread out in the water like kelp. Were they in on the plan too?

The music stopped and The Proprietor came out on stage.

Jordan frowned, this was unusual. The Proprietor was a back-room kind of man, a stick-to-the-shadows manipulator. But there he was in the spotlight, making a speech about the success of the club. Jordan's stomach knotted, why tonight of all nights? When the girls were planning something? What on Earth had possessed The Proprietor to do this?

Violet and Lily, who was dripping wet, walked the stage behind him, their eyes flashing in the reflected light. Both were stark naked and gorgeous.

Jordan saw a peculiar shine to Lily's skin. Violet seemed to be glowing slightly.

They put their hands on The Proprietor's shoulders. He smiled and announced them, said they'd be doing a special performance.

"Not quite," Violet said, her eyes on the floor as if she was too nervous to meet his gaze.

"We have something more in mind for you," Lily said. She ran her hand down the front of The Proprietor's shiny white shirt, caressing his pot belly. Water gushed out from behind the buttons, pouring on stage. The Proprietor's eyes bulged and he clutched at his throat.

Violet spun around, her hands made complicated movements in the air, as if she was playing an invisible instrument. Flowers bloomed on the stage and wild creepers ran rampant, growing in seconds to huge ropes of vegetation.

"That's our cue," the stag night guy said to Jordan.

Jordan was transfixed by the events on the stage, his mouth opening and shutting but no sound was coming out. "We don't have time for you to panic, just come on." The stag guy yanked him with a tight grip on his arm. Jordan stumbled to his feet but paused there looking around. The other men from party were taking off their coats and hoodies, revealing leather armour embossed with gold. The image of a stag with huge antlers was displayed on their chests.

"What?" Jordan looked at his drink; he must have been drugged again.

"Just come alright?" The youth tugged his arm again and Jordan blinked. At the door stood Angelo, a mountain of angry, solid flesh.

"This won't work," Jordan said. He was terrified now; the world didn't make any sense at all. The three stag night men in the lead drew swords, glistening and impossible. Their swords moved so fast Jordan couldn't make sense of it, but there was blood and Angelo crumpling to the ground, a confused look on his face.

Horrified, and barely breathing, Jordan turned back to the stage, wondering what had happened to the girls.

Violet and Lily tipped The Proprietor's body into one of the mermaid tanks. He wasn't moving. The other girls were nowhere to be seen.

"What's happening?" Jordan shouted. He wasn't even sure who he was asking at this point, people were moving everywhere, the tables and chairs upturned.

"We're getting you out, like I promised." The youth took off his baseball cap and Cherry's auburn hair tumbled down.

"But the ankle monitor," Jordan said. He pointed at his skinny ankle.

"Better cut that off." Cherry drew a sword that was as silver as the moonlight coming in the door. The club's usual low lights cut off completely. The vines, Jordan thought, the vines must have got into the mains. He flinched as Cherry slashed the sword down towards his leg, braced for the pain.

The ankle monitor fell off his ankle in two pieces. He looked up at Cherry with relief. "Thank you."

"Don't thank me now. Just get out of the building." Jordan and Cherry ran hand in hand out of the strip club, which was now flooded and mostly jungle. The other patrons were nowhere to be seen.

"Why are you doing this?" Jordan said, struggling to catch his breath.

"They wouldn't free us without a price," Cherry said. "Just us girls wasn't enough for them. I had to promise them something."

They ran, through the chill of the night, fresh air like Jordan hadn't breathed in what felt like a hundred years. His heart pounded.

Two blocks away the group stopped. The knights formed a ring around Cherry and Jordan.

"What are they? What are you?" Jordan said.

"Fairies," Cherry said. "They're fairy knights. The royal guard of the Twilight Court, they agreed to help us."

"Thank you so much for freeing me," Jordan said, he tried to sound formal. He even attempted a small bow, although he was still breathless, tripping over his words. "I really appreciate it. Seriously, I don't know how I would have got out on my own."

"You wouldn't have. And you probably won't want to thank me." Cherry sheathed her sword again and looked Jordan in the eyes. Her expression had become hard and distant. "We saved your life."

Jordan shivered. The wind was more than chilly, it was freezing. "Yes, thank you. I'll just be going." He turned to leave.

"No." One of the stag knights put his hand in the middle of Jordan's chest and pushed him back.

"No, don't you see?" Cherry moved closer, and hooked a finger under Jordan's chin, forcing his eyes to look into her bright, sparkling eyes. "We saved your life. That means we own your life. You'll come with us, now."

One of the smaller stag knights threw some powder from his pocket into the air.

The powder coalesced in the air and formed a sparkling golden door.

Cherry let go of Jordan, bowed to the door, and turned the handle.

On the other side of the door was another world. One full of pools, orchards, clinging vines, dancing bodies and flowers.

Jordan could see so many strange kinds of flowers, more kinds than he could name.

"Come on, J-Baby, we want to see how you watch these dancers."

A hand on the small of his back propelled him through the door and into eternity.

MORE POETRY

3^{.4} I tear into my skin with my fingernails
lever my ribs open
it hurts
but I've learned to keep
quiet when I'm in pain
hold back the tears
you've labelled my tears
as emotional manipulation

I LEVER my ribs open one by one
    there's my heart
    my lungs
    my esophagus
    my intestines

HAVE a play
    do what you want

it doesn't matter as long as
you're happy

Almost Too Much

In my dream this morning you were too close, too affectionate
    I strained to escape
    Trapped in the force of your desire
    Later, I saw your ghost
    In an innocent stranger on the street
    The same look – pale, big eyes searching
    Shoulders rounded, trying to take up less space
    Beautiful and flinching
    I remembered the way you used me. How you drew out
my love
    Took what you wanted
    Then turned away to a new target
    A new distraction
    I cried so hard

I've carved a space out of
    Myself each time I was hurt
    And now I'm secure,
    Loved,
    Supported,
    And I face the hardest task
    Of all, finding the me
    That's left over
    Filling up the gaping nothingness
    With light — healing — restoring
    My loving, optimistic true self

In spite of what you did

Overheard

I'M USED TO SUFFERING. I live in a house with you in it
    Yeah, get in there, show 'em what you got
    Whoa! Look at that wall!
    ~ tuneless whistling ~
    He was choking on it, eh?
    It was in Uranus, somewhere in that vicinity
    He doesn't know much, you know

Lucky Number Five

I step onto ice, not knowing how
    Thick or thin
    This could be a breeze
    Or it could be freezing death
    My patched-up heart wants to try

It's been lied to, shattered
    My heart has survived indifference
    It was endured disappointments
    Beyond measure
    Aching and breaking and tears
    Anyone sensible would stay on
    Solid ground
    No one has ever accused me of
    Being sensible
    When we studied love in First Year
    PSYCH 101

My friends laughed "this will be Jamie's favourite subject"
    Lost in the thrill of my first boyfriend, they were right
    I plant my foot on the slippery surface
    Hold my breath
    And start my walk towards you

Career Change

After years in office buildings,
    Data stored in servers
    Humming softly, in counterpoint
    To the air conditioning
    (which is always set low
    Because the gym bros are louder than the women)

After years of making myself
    Try and care about arbitrary deadlines
    About pieces of code going out
    This day
    Or that day

There's something satisfied deep in
    The soul of me
    To unlock the shop door with a key
    To sweep the leaves out of the entranceway
    As cars commute past
    I flip the sign from closed
    To open

To mind a shop of physical books
    Things I can touch
    A simple job
    My mind can ease, my heart thrums joy
    I don't have to pretend to care about this

Have you got?

Rather sophisticated books on
    War, politics, train engines,
    That sort of thing?

Jimmy Barnes' autobiography, the second volume
    Magic eye books?

A book about a woman
    Travelling in Africa, I can't recall the name

Anything by Shirley Maclaine?

A book about how all
    The USA's problems started in the
    Last seventy years

I don't remember the author

A book of photos of early
    New Zealand colonial kitchens?

Books about the Malayan Emergency?

There was in art book
    In the window
    A few weeks back
    Do you still have it?
    I don't know who it was about, or what it looked like

21

TOBY'S TATTOO

"It's a memorial, of sorts."

"Sorry for your loss," the tattooist said in a detached way, already distracted.

He was getting the tattoo to mourn, that much was true. He'd lost his best friend.

More than that, the love of his life.

Micah.

His fingers long and slender, playing a love song for Toby on the antique piano.

She finished drawing on Toby's arm and turned away to start sterilising needles.

"It's alright," Toby said. "It's better this way."

She nodded, although Toby thought he sounded like he was rejoicing the death of a friend, of true love.

Not that Micah was dead.

The last Toby had heard he was a guest at some music festival on the huge ship where the Bahamas had been, before the oceans rose.

It had been all over social media. Plastered so that Toby couldn't avoid reading the news, seeing the ticket prices. The golden child, Micah, playing his songs perfectly.

The very songs he'd written for Toby.

Or, well.

Maybe some of them had been written for the previous Toby. Or the one before that... It was impossible to know, and he never would. He had to let that go.

The tattooist started to work.

Toby's jaw clenched, he could blame it on the needle, this tension, but really it was the train of thought.

Micah never told him, definitively, how many had come before. Which number iteration Toby was. Did it even matter? He asked himself, but he always replied back the same way. Of course it mattered. He needed to know who he was, who his ancestors were. What parts of him were his own.

But.

He was free now. And this tattoo? It was insurance.

Evidence that whatever Micah, or his bio-fabricating mad scientist of a father did, they couldn't erase him.

He would always be unique.

If they ever tracked him down, or worse, if the next iteration of Toby found him...

Time flew by. His jaw clenched and his teeth ached, ignoring the needles as best he could.

Finally, she held up a mirror so Toby could see it, red and raw but beautifully indelible.

A bird, flying free of a cage in bright sunshine yellow.

"What do you think?"

"Perfect."

22

ONE LAST JOB

"Hey, you're Viggo Valinar of the Veracious Vale, right?"

Viggo sighed. He had been walking for some hours, so it was something of a relief to pause, turn around, and regard the approaching person. They were young - with short black hair, brand new leather leggings and shiny, unbroken-in boots. A bow and quiver of arrows were slung on their back alongside a pack and bedroll.

"Who's asking?"

"I'm Blake, I use they and them pronouns," Blake said.

"What do you want?"

"To join you. I heard talk at the inn that you were going after the dragon and I want to help-"

"Nope." Viggo turned to go.

"Okay, but you're just one guy and it's a whole entire dragon. I'm good with my bow and I have a dagger in my pack, I'm sure you could use my help."

Viggo shook his head, looked back. "Dagger's no good in your pack, you need to have it close to hand in a fight."

Blake's smile lit their face up with incredible hope. "Yes, see? There's so much I can learn from you. Please, let me come with?"

"Nope." Viggo turned to look up the path, the direction he was heading. "I work alone, and this is my last job."

He started to walk again, a little pleased with how bad ass and dramatic the end to the conversation had been.

In a moment the archer was trotting alongside him.

"I said no."

"That's fine, you said no, I heard you and I respect that," Blake said. "But it just so happens, I'm walking this way, too." Blake grinned, showing all of their teeth. Clearly thrilled with their own cleverness.

Viggo ignored Blake and their relentless attempts at conversation for the next few hours.

It was mid-afternoon when something caught Viggo's eye and he veered to the left of the path, knelt and examined the clue he had been looking for.

"What's that?" Blake leaned over him, a little too close.

"Charred twig," Viggo said. He picked it up, turned it this way and that and then looked skywards. "Yep, the topmost branches of the tree are burned up."

Blake shifted their weight and followed his gaze. "Huh, yes. So that means the dragon came this way, right? That we're on the right track?"

"*I* am on the right track, *you* are not involved in this dragon hunt" Viggo said. He stood and fixed Blake a look that had, in the past, made an orc warlord reconsider his plans to attack. Viggo had worked hard to make his glare as baleful as humanly possible.

Today, it failed.

Blake smiled back guilelessly, and Viggo worried that he had lost his edge in partial retirement.

"I am hunting the dragon completely separately from you."

Viggo sighed mightily, all the weariness of the road, the irritating companions and the dull ache in his joints weighing him down.

~

BLAKE WAS, predictably, still beside him when the sun began to dip towards the horizon.

Viggo left the track to find a suitable glade to make camp for the night, Blake dumped his pack and bedroll down and went off into the woods.

Viggo reluctantly accepted the pheasant Blake returned with, and together they prepared it, and roasted it over the campfire Viggo had built to share for supper.

"So, you're the legendary hero, Viggo Valinar, huh?"

"Mhm. The pheasant's good, fat," Viggo said.

"Just needs some roast vegetables to make it perfect," Blake said. They sounded wistful, Viggo thought perhaps he'd successfully changed the subject, but then, "I'd heard you'd retired, that's what everyone was saying."

"One last quest," Viggo said. He sucked the last pieces of meat off a pheasant bone and then tossed it into the fire. "Favour for the town mayor."

"Yeah?" Blake blinked at him over the flames. "So, if you weren't out adventuring, what were you doing with yourself?"

Viggo considered lying. He really did. But if Blake had heard the stories of his long thirty years of adventuring, and of his retirement, then they had almost certainly heard of the bakery.

"I was making bread, teaching myself cakes, selling the results."

Blake's eyes widened. "It's true? I didn't think it could be. I'd heard so many tales of your exploits, of the monster slaying and the freeing of the oppressed and so on, and then to hear what you were doing now was selling the land's most charred bread?"

Viggo shuffled back from the light of the fire to hide the flush that beset his cheeks. "I'm still learning. S'not as easy as it looks."

A noise in the nearby trees had both of them on high alert in an instant.

"Good evening, friends," a voice floated over the night air, breathy and low. Blake's bow was strung and an arrow notched in a moment, Viggo's sword was in his hand as he stood to face the intruder. He listened hard, aware of any other noises. Was this new person part of a group? Were they already surrounded? It wouldn't be the first time that had happened.

A figure moved out of the forest, hands raised in a gesture of peace. They wore a simple white shirt and brown trousers. "I am Sorrel, a simple man of the forest, and I wish to warm myself by your fire, if I may. I am unarmed and I mean no ill-will."

Viggo didn't lower his sword.

"How long have you been watching us?"

"No time at all." The stranger, Sorrel, moved forward enough that Viggo saw his eyes were a strange, unsettling grey colour, and his hair was long, pale, and slightly green. Viggo had met many elves in his time, and when the stranger pushed a lock of his long hair behind a pointed air, Viggo decided that elf was what this man must be. It explained his silent approach, and appearance.

"I have wine, if you'd like to share your fire, I would happily pour it for you. I also have fresh berries, I believe your kind-" Sorrel cut himself off awkwardly, but looked hopefully at the two of them. "Uh, enjoy berries."

Viggo had heard no other sounds, although if they were surrounded by wood elves with ill-intent there was precious little they would hear, or could do to save themselves. He was used to trusting his gut, and his gut said that Sorrel meant just what he said.

Vigo lowered his sword, Blake lowered their bow.

"Come, Sorrel, there's plenty of room," Viggo said. "The stars know I could do with a change of conversation."

Sorrel smiled wide, pulled a sling from their back to their front and settled with inhuman grace beside Viggo.

"Your reputation precedes you into this forest, Valinar," Sorrel said. His voice was almost hypnotic, low, breathy and slightly rasping.

"Just Viggo, please," Viggo said. "I am retired. Most of the time."

Sorrel pulled out a wineskin and a wooden cup.

"Retired, mm?" Sorrel poured wine into the wooden cup, then into Viggo's battered old tin one, and into Blake's brand new tin one. "I expect you are looking for the dragon?"

Viggo nodded and sniffed the wine. Thirty long years of adventuring had sharpened his nose to the presence of poison, and his charmed bracelet would glow if there was harmful magic present. It didn't, there wasn't. He sipped the wine and hummed.

"This is very good," he said. He looked up at Sorrel but found it hard to meet his piercing gaze for any length of time. "Thank you."

"Anything for the famed Ser Valinor, sorry, Ser Viggo," Sorrel said. His voice warmed a little, and Viggo felt a curious shiver go up his spine. He took another drink.

"Just Viggo."

Blake looked between them and chuckled. "So, Sorrel, what have you heard about Viggo?"

Sorrel's expression brightened. "I have heard so many fine tales from travelling bards. I believe my favourite is the one about the dungeons of Argonath and his battles with the skeletons within."

"That is a great one," Blake said. "But have you heard of the Northern Princess's birthday party? Viggo was there, and it was gatecrashed by bounty hunters…"

Viggo groaned, downed his wine, and shuffled back from the fire. He rolled himself in his bedding and tried to ignore the sounds of Blake and Sorrel sharing tales of his past.

～

SORREL WOKE him a few hours before dawn. "Blake is asleep, Ser Viggo," he said. "I need to take my leave now, it is your turn to watch."

Viggo was surprised that Sorrel had woken him without triggering his attack reflex. His hand was relaxed on the hilt of his sword. It meant that some part of him trusted Sorrel, which was exceedingly strange since he barely knew the elf. He sat up and nodded. "Of course."

"There's a fine cave on your trail," Sorrel said. "You should reach it by sundown if you make a good pace. It's North East, towards the mountain. The trees on the way are marked with three lines, old ranger markings. They will lead you right to it."

Viggo narrowed his eyes. Everything about Sorrel was confusing. "Very well, thank you."

"Be safe." Sorrel leaned in, and placed a soft kiss on the top of Viggo's head before smiling, turning and hurrying away into the darkness.

"What the fuck was that?" Viggo whispered.

The kiss in itself was strange, for certain, but Viggo had visited enough different lands and peoples to know that cultures varied, and perhaps a kiss was normal for Sorrel.

What he didn't understand was why the kiss had made him feel warm all over. He shook his head and pulled himself fully out of his bedding, ready to fulfil watch duty while Blake snored on the other side of the fire.

Viggo tuned out the snores, and listened to the forest noises around him.

THE NEXT DAY, the charred branches led North East. They abandoned the common path, and made their way through the forest proper. Sure enough Viggo started to see trees with three lines chipped into the bark. The ranger markings Sorrel had mentioned. It irked him a little, to be constantly reminded of

Sorrel, and his charmingly soothing voice, and the kiss on the head, which kept on bringing the slightest of warmth to Viggo's cheeks.

After noon, Viggo decided that anything was worth a break from his thoughts and struck up conversation with Blake.

"So, this is your first quest, isn't it?"

Blake looked over at him, startled. "Yes, how did you know?"

"Brand new boots, cup, kit," Viggo said. "Why this one? Most would try and work up to a dragon."

"Well, you," Blake said. "You're the greatest hero of our age, everyone knows that."

Viggo grunted. "It's not all it's cracked up to be."

"But it's so cool, everyone has heard of you, everyone tells stories about the amazing things you've done. You must have had so many wonderful days and nights."

"What people don't tell stories of is mostly what I remember," Viggo said. "Bruises that take days to heal, broken sleep for weeks on end, blisters and sunburn and aches that never fully go away. Making hard decisions, which you can never be sure are right..." he sighed heavily.

Blake sighed. "I've only been at it a day and a half and I already have blisters."

"New boots," Viggo said. "Here, there's a stream ahead. Soak the leather and when it's drying put them on again, they'll mould better to your foot then."

THEY REACHED AN ABANDONED BEAR cave just before sunset, it was in the low hills that surrounded the mountain the dragon was said to roost in. Viggo wanted to find some reason to not use it, but there was nothing. It was empty of rats or remains, it had a good vantage point on any approaches and a clear space out front where they could make a fire. Sorrel had been right.

Viggo went for firewood while Blake hunted for dinner.

Viggo was lighting the fire when Sorrel emerged from the tree-line. Once again dressed simply, with a sling over one shoulder.

Viggo sat back on his haunches and regarded the elf. "You again."

"You found the cave, I'm glad of it," Sorrel said.

"You were following us? Are you tracking the dragon as well?" Viggo had more or less made peace with never seeing the stranger again, and now here he was. Viggo foolishly, wondered if he might get another kiss.

"I'm not following you, I live nearby," Sorrel said. He pulled his sling to the front and produced some freshly dug carrots, parsnips and three large potatoes. "I thought you might appreciate these, to roast in the embers."

"That..." Viggo nodded slowly. "Yeah, those look great, they'll be good for dinner."

Blake returned with three trout on a string. "Oh, hey Sorrel! I found this pool nearby full of fish, the river comes straight down off the mountain, so it's cold, but we could bathe in there, too."

Viggo looked between Sorrel, who had elegantly folded his legs and settled beside the fire as if he'd always been there, and Blake, who set about filleting the already cleaned fish. It seemed, despite his intention to carry out this mission alone, he had two companions. Although he wasn't at all sure if Sorrel would be around during the day come the morning.

He wanted to prod Blake about the weirdness of Sorrel turning up again, or to complain about how he didn't need assistance on this quest, but he found he couldn't voice the complaint. It was a warm, pleasant evening, and the fire had caught beautifully and he discovered he wasn't annoyed at all. He felt a curious sense of serenity instead.

Later, when the stars had come out, and the last of the fish had been eaten, Blake wiped off his hands and nodded to Sorrel.

"Why don't you tell us a story from around these parts? There must be some good local tales."

Sorrel raised his eyebrows and nodded. "Well, I moved to

these parts fairly recently, but I suppose I could tell you a story from my people… although, it might sound rather strange."

"Go ahead," Viggo said. He settled more comfortably against the bundle of bedding he'd been leaning on. "We need to pass the time somehow, and I like good stories."

Sorrel's cheeks coloured slightly and he ducked his head. "I shall try and tell it the best way I can."

Sorrel's story was indeed curious. Dealing with aspects of elven life that Viggo didn't comprehend - a certain fascination with fire, and the weather in the mountains. The tribe Sorrel hailed from sounded very unlike the forest elves he'd met before.

A suspicion kindled in the back of Viggo's mind, but he didn't speak it. Instead he listened, and let Sorrel's soothingly low, breathy voice wash over him.

When he was done, Blake told a story from his childhood, and before it was Viggo's turn, he yawned and asked who would take first watch. Sorrel insisted that the two of them sleep and he would watch first.

Viggo woke with the sunrise, startled and feeling like he'd slept far too long. Sorrel sat with his back to the last smouldering embers, and Blake was bundled in their bedroll, only a nose visible.

"You stayed up all night," Viggo accused. He sat up. "You should have woken me."

"No," Sorrel said. "You have a long, hard day ahead of you. I wanted you to be well rested." He turned, and smiled, and in the dawn light his hair seemed to spark like the curious blue and green centre of a roaring fire. Viggo stood, shook out his bedroll and tried not to think too hard about how handsome Sorrel was.

"Still. I could have taken a watch."

Sorrel was beside him in an instant. "If you would allow people to help you more, perhaps you could be happier," he said. His voice was soft, barely more than a whisper. "Perhaps you wouldn't burn so much bread, if you had accepted help from someone who knew how to bake."

Viggo grunted and turned away. "I'm too old to apprentice to a baker."

Sorrel hummed. Viggo turned back to say something about the smug smile on his face, but before he could Sorrel leaned in and kissed him on the lips. It was brief, a peck, fleeting, but Viggo's lips tingled, and he was utterly aware of the softness of Sorrel's lips, and the way his body instantly yearned for more.

"I'll see you tonight," Sorrel said. "Unless you lose your way."

"You aren't-" Viggo asked, but Sorrel was already hurrying away from the fire. Viggo's knees threatened to buckle, so he sat back down and put on a pot of rice porridge for breakfast.

THE DAY WAS INDEED hard and long. The path gave away to difficult to navigate sections of scree and rocky outcroppings that had to be clambered over. Viggo watched Blake, half concerned they would decide this part of the adventure was too hard and turn back, and half concerned they'd hurt themself in the trying.

Blake didn't complain, simply attacked each challenge with cheerful good humour and relatively nimble feet. Both of them had setbacks of course, scree would send them sliding back down, or a rock would crumble under a handhold, but Blake would smile it off.

"Not that one, then," they'd say. Then approach it in a different way. The sun beat down on them both, harsh and unrelenting but every now and then Blake would turn and look out at the view and exclaim.

"It almost makes me want to become a bard, you know? It's so beautiful, and you can see so much from up this high. Maybe I should try writing poems."

"Maybe," Viggo said. He looked out over the vista and he had to admit it was heartening, Blake's enthusiasm was almost enough for Viggo to ignore the ache in his bad left knee, or the way his back protested if he stretched his arms too high up over his head.

They climbed the mountain, and finally arrived at the vast cavern, which had a small plume of smoke trailing out of it and up into the sky.

Despite the sun, the air was colder up there, and it chilled the sweat soaked clothes on Viggo's back.

"This is it," Viggo said. He pulled his sword from his back and undid the wrappings that had protected it during the climb, set his pack down and rolled his shoulders out.

Beside him, Blake set their pack down, strung their bow and readied their arrows.

"Aim for the spaces between scales," Viggo said. "Particularly under the throat, they're a little softer there."

Blake nodded. Their rosy complexion had paled. "Do you really think we can do this?"

Viggo took a look at Blake, and then down at himself. A past-it old adventurer, years too late to be prime, and a new recruit who had never faced anything like this before.

"Absolutely."

He approached the cave on silent feet and lowered his voice to a barest whisper. "It should be sleeping this time of day, our best tactic is to corner it in the cave and take it sleeping."

Blake's eyes were round but there was a steel set to their jaw. They nodded and followed Viggo.

Viggo had only got two steps inside when there was a loud, low growl that shook the cave walls. "Get BACK!"

Viggo pushed Blake back and around the corner of the cave opening before a huge wave of roasting-hot fire erupted from the cave.

"Holy fuck!" Blake shout-whispered. "Not asleep then?"

"Not asleep," Viggo said. A moment later the huge head of the dragon emerged from the cave, looking this way and that. Its scales were a fine, sapphire blue that would camouflage it with the sky beautifully. Its eyes were green, the green of the centre of a roaring campfire.

Viggo's breath caught.

The dragon seemed to barely fit in the cave, it squeezed its shoulders out slowly, with some effort. Viggo pushed Blake further back, but the ledge the cave entrance stood on only went so far.

The dragon heard their scuffling and ponderously turned its head. "Want my gold, eh? You can't have it. If you would leave with your skins intact now is the time."

Viggo looked deep into the green eyes and nodded once. There was no way he and Blake could take on such a huge creature, especially without the element of surprise. "Just on our way out, Ser Dragon."

"Good." The dragon flopped down onto the flat ledge and folded its paws under its chin. The impact of it hitting the ground jostled them both and Blake clung to Viggo's arm hard enough to bruise. "Mind you take your things, leave any gold."

"Don't have any gold to leave," Blake said. "I'm so sorry, your eminence."

"Mmm."

So, they scuttled around the massive beast, collected their packs and made their way back down the mountain. They stopped at a smaller cave, roughly half the way back down and regrouped.

"That dragon could have killed us!" Blake had apparently been holding it together and now they were panicking, voice cracking. "It was so close, and its fangs were so large!"

"Yeah," Viggo said. "It could have, and they were."

"I've never been that close to death before, oh my stars, I could have died..." Blake crouched on the ground, hands rooted in their hair and eyes wide, staring. "I loved it!"

Viggo couldn't stop the gales of laughter. He knew exactly what Blake meant. The thrill, the chase, and then the sudden confrontation with one's own mortality. Beating it back, coming out alive?

It was why he had adventured for as long as he had after all.

His stomach hurt from the laughter, and he braced one forearm across himself and slid down the cave wall to collapse on his arse, letting the giggles take him.

Blake joined in, and the two of them had a wild, raucous laugh.

Finally, Viggo pulled himself together. "Let's see if our mysterious friend can be lured by the campfire," Viggo said. "Because I suspect-"

Before he'd even left the small cave to find firewood, Sorrel was approaching from below.

"Good afternoon," Sorrel called out. "I saw some fire on the mountaintop, how did it go?"

Viggo barked out another laugh. Feeling giddy and bold.

"You tell me, Sorrel," he said. "As I rather suspect you were there."

"You were... he was... What?" Blake asked, eyes wide. "Sorrel wasn't there."

Sorrel looked first defensive and then embarrassed.

"He's the dragon," Viggo said. "S'why we're still alive, am I right?"

Sorrel's gaze flicked between the two of them, a rabbit caught in a trap, looking for an escape. Then his expression softened, and he smiled.

"I'm just such a huge fan, Ser Viggo."

"What? What does that even mean?" Blake asked. They folded their arms and looked at Viggo. "You knew?"

"Well, there were quite a few hints," Viggo said. "But I wasn't sure until the dragon didn't eat us."

"I'd never eat a human!" Sorrel's hand flew to his chest in outrage. Perhaps it was offensive to imply dragons ate people.

"Well, most dragons would have killed us, if not *eaten* us,"

Viggo said. "But you expected us, put on a show, and then let us go unharmed. That's unheard of."

"I'm sorry, I just wanted…" Sorrel breathed out and smiled. "I wanted to see you in action, and it was desperately thrilling, the whole journey. I especially love the whole grudging master teaching the young, eager apprentice twist. I have to admit I didn't expect it, but it was entertaining."

"You pulled me out of retirement so that you could watch me hunt you?" Viggo knew he should be annoyed, but the traces of giggles were still present, and he was tired, and he couldn't muster the energy to be angry at this handsome, strange dragon-man.

"Yes. And so that we could get to know one another," Sorrel said.

"But why? Just to watch us? That seems like so much effort to go to, you stole sheep and burned up bandits, and…" Blake trailed off.

"The sheep are fine," Sorrel said. He made his way to the entrance of the cave and in silent agreement they all sat down. "I've been keeping them on the far side of the forest, and I will return them all, now that you're done with your quest."

Viggo rubbed his hands over his face. "So you'll stop being a menace?"

"Yes," Sorrel said. "Only, I'd like you to consider my proposal."

"You're proposing?" Blake's eyes nearly bulged out of their head.

"Well, not like that, not yet," Sorrel said. "I wanted to suggest that you employ me at your bakery. By all reports your bread always comes out burned. That means you don't know how to work the fires to make a proper heated oven. I can help with that! Leave the fires and the oven to me, and you can concentrate on the mixing and kneading and dealing with customers."

There was silence for a few long moments while Viggo tried to understand what Sorrel had done, and what he was offering to do.

"You want to help in my bakery? He asked, finally, somehow this aspect of the conversation refused to make sense to him. The word 'yet' kept repeating in his mind.

"Yes," Sorrel said. "Very much."

"You want to tend the ovens so that my loaves aren't burned."

"Exactly."

Viggo laughed again. When was the last time he'd laughed so much in such a short time? He couldn't remember.

"Fine. Yes, why the fuck not? I can go back to being retired, and maybe my bakery will make a name for itself beyond the burning."

Sorrel beamed and flung himself at Viggo, wrapping his arms tight around him. "Thank you! I love you! I'll be so good at it, your bakery will be the most famous in the land!"

Viggo felt his entire head flush at Sorrel's words. He tentatively raised a hand to pat Sorrel's back. "Yes. Well. Good."

Blake met Viggo's eyes and grinned wide. "Sorrel might be just what you need, in more ways than one. I'm going to go hunt for dinner and give you two lovebirds some alone time." With that they were gone, and Viggo and Sorrel were alone. Sorrel settled in Viggo's lap and looked at him with beautiful green eyes.

"Are you alright? Your cheeks are very pink."

"Yes, um, you said you loved me, humans don't usually do that with people they don't know well," he said.

"Oh," Sorrel said. He tilted his head to one side. "Sorry."

Viggo looped his arms around Sorrel's waist, feeling bold, about to take on a dragon. "It's all right, I liked hearing it, and I like you too. I don't know about love, that usually takes some time, at least in the stories, but … I like the idea of us making a life in the bakery."

Sorrel made a soft happy chirping noise, and crashed his lips against Viggo's. Viggo returned the kiss with a little more finesse, and pulled Sorrel closer.

~

A FEW MONTHS LATER, Blake stopped in at the bakery to say goodbye.

"It's all happening," they said. Their boots were worn in now. "I've found four others to join me, and we're heading out just before dawn tomorrow."

"That's wonderful news." Viggo shuffled around the front counter to give Blake a warm hug. "I'll give you some wayfarer bread, and some cakes just for the first day."

"Thanks, dad!" Blake said, beaming.

"For the last time, I'm not your father," Viggo said. His cheeks pinked again, and he knew Blake had noticed.

"You're my adventurer dad," Blake said. "And you always will be. How's my dragon dad?"

"Sorrel, my dear!" Viggo turned to call out.

In a moment, Sorrel peered around the corner, hair tied back and covered with a gingham headscarf. "Oh, Blake, my favourite child!"

"You're as bad as each other," Viggo muttered. He went to pack up some bread and treats for Blake.

Sorrel and Blake hugged and exchanged a hushed and fast conversation. Viggo ignored this, they often spoke about him in such a way and he'd learned he didn't want to hear what Blake asked, or the detail with which Sorrel answered.

One of his regulars came in and ordered her usual: coffee cake and a loaf of sourdough, and by the time Viggo had packed it up and taken payment, Blake and Sorrel were both watching him with fond smiles.

"Here you go, you absolute nightmare." Viggo shoved the bundle towards Blake. "Be safe, and remember to keep your weapons at hand."

"Thanks Dad." Blake leaned over the counter to kiss Viggo on the cheek, and although he made a show of grumbling, Viggo leaned in and kissed Blake's cheek, and patted his shoulder.

"Take this," Sorrel said, pressing something small and blue into Blake's hand. "It's one of my scales, it should bring you a bit of luck, and if you do that spell I taught you, you can summon me, if you need me."

Blake gave Sorrel a big hug. Sorrel slipped back around the counter and under Viggo's arm and they waved Blake off together. Viggo squeezed Sorrel tighter than usual against him and blinked back a tear, his throat suddenly sore.

"They grow up so fast, don't they?"

Sorrel pecked him on the cheek and then let go. "I need to make sure the teacakes don't burn, love."

Viggo wrung his hands in his apron and watched the direction Blake had gone, feeling sad, worried and yes, a little jealous it wasn't him hitting the road to adventure. But then the mayor came in for a slice of peach pie, and a half dozen sugar cookies for his daughter's birthday, and Viggo felt settled once more.

NOTE FROM THE AUTHOR:

I hope you've enjoyed this collection. It's been decades in the making, and I left out a couple of short stories that needed to stay a couple of decades in the past...

If you enjoyed this book please do leave a review for it somewhere online. Reviews are the best way to recommend a book to another reader, and I really do appreciate you taking the time, even if it's just a single line.

Many of these short stories have been published on my substack in some form or another, please consider signing up to keep up with what's happening. You can find it here:

https://jamiedwrites.substack.com/

All of my other socials and links to my other books, etc can be found here:
https://linktr.ee/JamieDSands

Which Tree, A Summon a Howling, previously published in charity anthologies

End of the Rainbow previously published in *Baby Teeth*

Unconsented Additions previously published in *This is Too Tense!*

Rise of the Kaiju Fighters previously published in *Rise*

Toby's Tattoo previously published in *Ink*

Waiheke Christmas previously published in *Jingle Spells – a Witchy Fiction Christmas Anthology*

One Last Job previously published in *Tales from the Tavern*

ALSO BY JAMIE SANDS